THE BOYHOOD OF THOR!

Writer: STAN LEE
Penciler: JACK KIRBY

Inkers: PAUL REINMAN, GEORGE BELL & CHIC STONE
Colorist: MATT MILLA
Letterer: ART SIMEK

Cover Artists: OLIVIER COIPEL, MARK MORALES
& LAURA MARTIN

Collection Editors: MARK D. BEAZLEY & CORY LEVINE
Assistant Editors: ALEX STARBUCK & NELSON RIBEIRO
Editor, Special Projects: JENNIFER GRÜNWALD
Senior Editor, Special Projects: JEFF YOUNGQUIST
SVP of Print & Digital Publishing Sales: DAVID GABRIEL
Research: JEPH YORK & DANA PERKINS
Select Art Reconstruction: TOM ZIUKO
Production: JERRON QUALITY COLOR & JOE FRONTIRRE
Book Designer: SPRING HOTELING

Editor In Chief: AXEL ALONSO
Chief Creative Officer: JOE QUESADA
Publisher: DAN BUCKLEY
Executive Producer: ALAN FINE

SPECIAL THANKS TO RALPH MACCHIO

Visit us at www.abdopublishing.com

Reinforced library bound editions published in 2014 by Spotlight, a division of the ABDO Group, PO Box 398166, Minneapolis, MN 55439. Spotlight produces high-quality reinforced library bound editions for schools and libraries. Published by agreement with Marvel Characters, Inc.

Printed in the United States of America, North Mankato, Minnesota.
042013
092013
♻ This book contains at least 10% recycled material.

MARVEL

marvel.com
© 2013 Marvel

Library of Congress Cataloging-in-Publication Data

Lee, Stan.
 The boyhood of Thor! / story by Stan Lee ; art by Jack Kirby.
    pages cm. -- (Thor, tales of Asgard)
 "Marvel."
 Summary: An adaptation, in graphic novel form, of comic books revealing the adventures of the Norse Gods and Thor before he came to Earth, featuring the godling Balder and how Odin made him invincible.
 ISBN 978-1-61479-170-6 (alk. paper)
 1. Thor (Norse deity)--Juvenile fiction. 2. Graphic novels. [1. Graphic novels. 2. Thor (Norse deity)--Fiction. 3. Mythology, Norse--Fiction.] I. Kirby, Jack, illustrator. II. Title.
 PZ7.S81712Boy 2013
 741.5'973--dc23
                                    2013005404

All Spotlight books are reinforced library bindings
and manufactured in the United States of America.

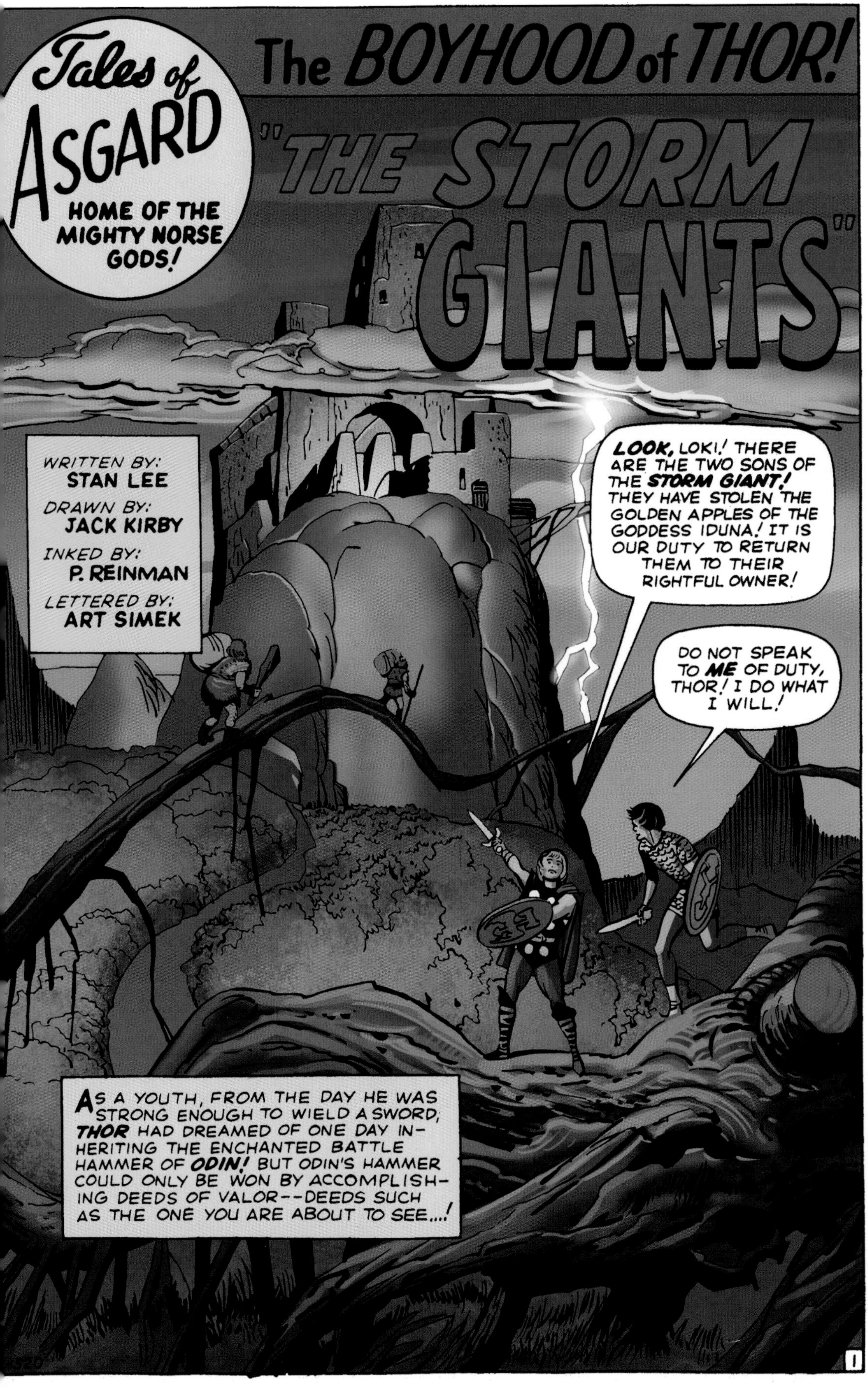
Tales of ASGARD
HOME OF THE MIGHTY NORSE GODS!
The BOYHOOD of THOR!
"THE STORM GIANTS"
WRITTEN BY: STAN LEE
DRAWN BY: JACK KIRBY
INKED BY: P. REINMAN
LETTERED BY: ART SIMEK
LOOK, LOKI! THERE ARE THE TWO SONS OF THE STORM GIANT! THEY HAVE STOLEN THE GOLDEN APPLES OF THE GODDESS IDUNA! IT IS OUR DUTY TO RETURN THEM TO THEIR RIGHTFUL OWNER!
DO NOT SPEAK TO ME OF DUTY, THOR! I DO WHAT I WILL!
AS A YOUTH, FROM THE DAY HE WAS STRONG ENOUGH TO WIELD A SWORD, THOR HAD DREAMED OF ONE DAY INHERITING THE ENCHANTED BATTLE HAMMER OF ODIN! BUT ODIN'S HAMMER COULD ONLY BE WON BY ACCOMPLISHING DEEDS OF VALOR--DEEDS SUCH AS THE ONE YOU ARE ABOUT TO SEE...!
1

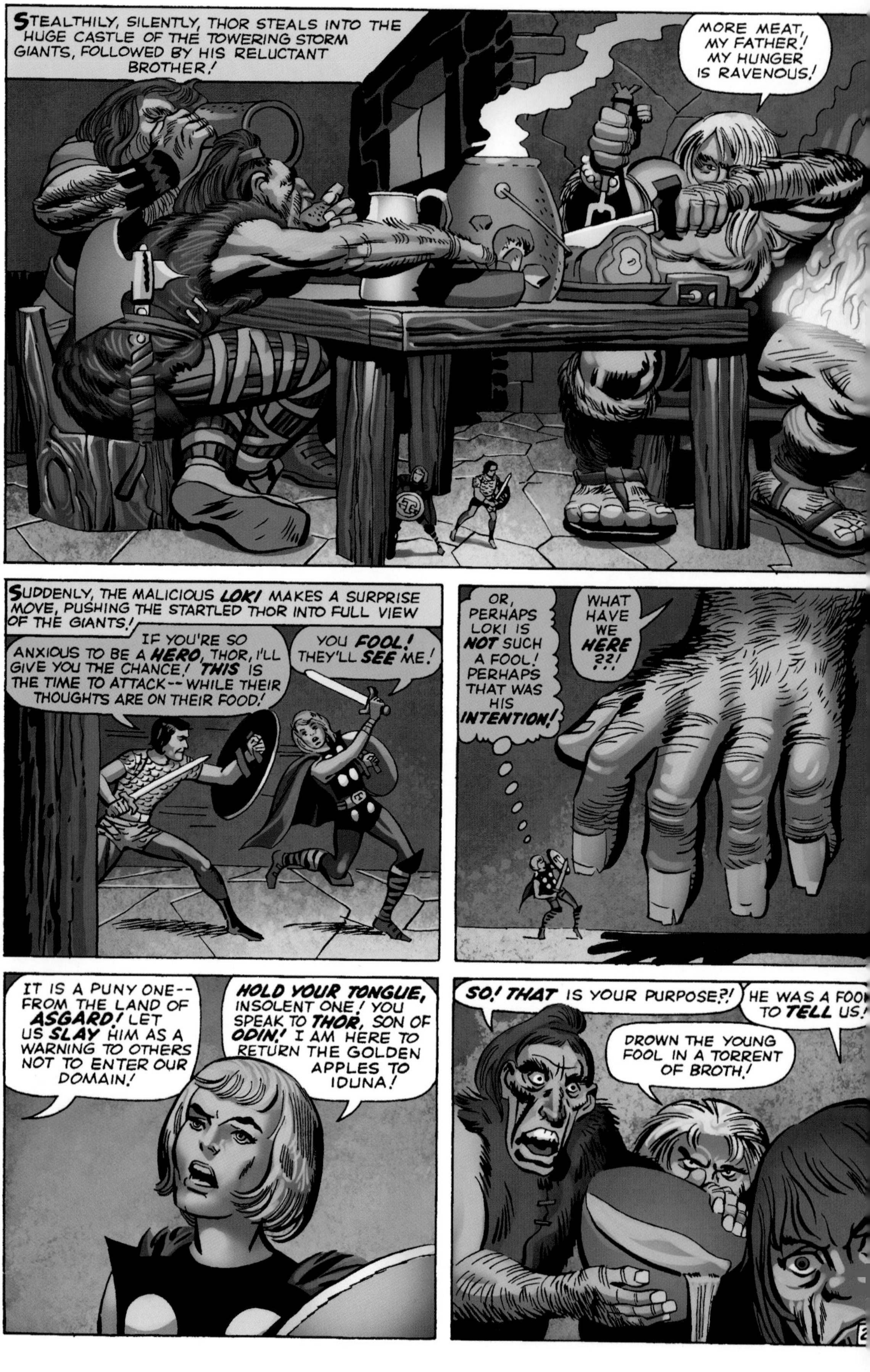

STEALTHILY, SILENTLY, THOR STEALS INTO THE HUGE CASTLE OF THE TOWERING STORM GIANTS, FOLLOWED BY HIS RELUCTANT BROTHER!
MORE MEAT, MY FATHER! MY HUNGER IS RAVENOUS!
SUDDENLY, THE MALICIOUS LOKI MAKES A SURPRISE MOVE, PUSHING THE STARTLED THOR INTO FULL VIEW OF THE GIANTS!
IF YOU'RE SO ANXIOUS TO BE A HERO, THOR, I'LL GIVE YOU THE CHANCE! THIS IS THE TIME TO ATTACK-- WHILE THEIR THOUGHTS ARE ON THEIR FOOD!
YOU FOOL! THEY'LL SEE ME!
WHAT HAVE WE HERE ??!
OR, PERHAPS LOKI IS NOT SUCH A FOOL! PERHAPS THAT WAS HIS INTENTION!
IT IS A PUNY ONE-- FROM THE LAND OF ASGARD! LET US SLAY HIM AS A WARNING TO OTHERS NOT TO ENTER OUR DOMAIN!
HOLD YOUR TONGUE, INSOLENT ONE! YOU SPEAK TO THOR, SON OF ODIN! I AM HERE TO RETURN THE GOLDEN APPLES TO IDUNA!
SO! THAT IS YOUR PURPOSE?!
HE WAS A FOO TO TELL US!
DROWN THE YOUNG FOOL IN A TORRENT OF BROTH!

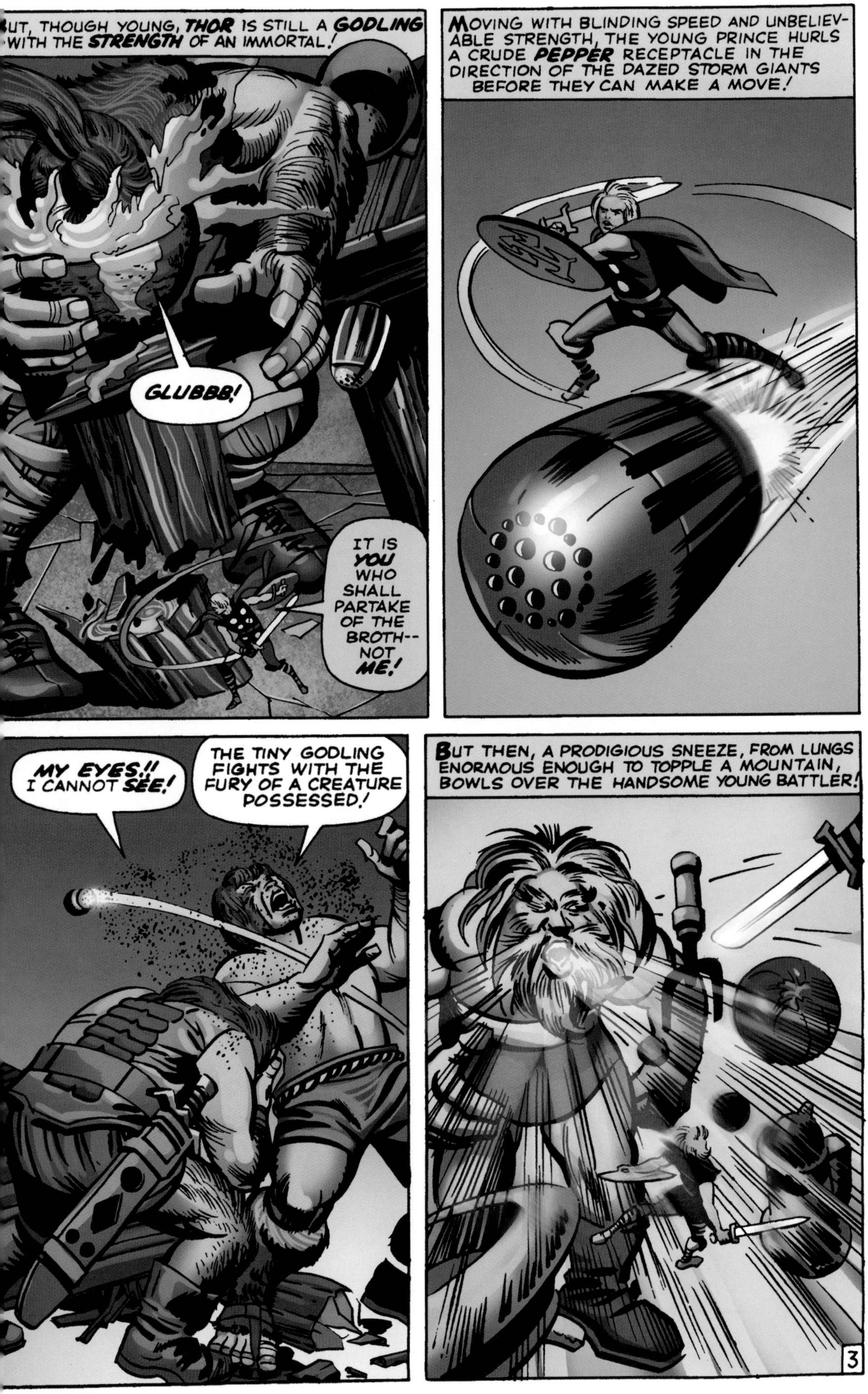
BUT, THOUGH YOUNG, THOR IS STILL A GODLING WITH THE STRENGTH OF AN IMMORTAL!
GLUBBB!
IT IS YOU WHO SHALL PARTAKE OF THE BROTH-- NOT ME!
MOVING WITH BLINDING SPEED AND UNBELIEVABLE STRENGTH, THE YOUNG PRINCE HURLS A CRUDE PEPPER RECEPTACLE IN THE DIRECTION OF THE DAZED STORM GIANTS BEFORE THEY CAN MAKE A MOVE!
MY EYES!! I CANNOT SEE!
THE TINY GODLING FIGHTS WITH THE FURY OF A CREATURE POSSESSED!
BUT THEN, A PRODIGIOUS SNEEZE, FROM LUNGS ENORMOUS ENOUGH TO TOPPLE A MOUNTAIN, BOWLS OVER THE HANDSOME YOUNG BATTLER!
3

AND, BEFORE THOR CAN REGAIN HIS BALANCE, HIS SWORD IS RENDERED USELESS BY A TITANIC FIST!

I'M *TRAPPED!*

HAH! SO *THIS* IS THE ONE WHO DARED DEFY US!

SEE HOW HELPLESS HE IS NOW!

PERHAPS I SHALL *KEEP* HIM AND WEAR HIM TIED TO MY BELT AS AN ORNAMENT.

BUT, AT THAT MOMENT, THE WILY LOKI, WHO HAS NOT YET BEEN SEEN, TOSSES A PILE OF WET LEAVES INTO THE HUGE, FLAMING FIREPLACE...

AND, WITHIN SECONDS, THICK CLOUDS OF BLINDING SMOKE FILL THE VAST CHAMBER!

THERE MUST BE *ANOTHER* TINY ONE HIDDEN AMONG US!

WAIT NO LONGER! *KILL* HIM! SLAY THEM *ALL!*

BUT, UNDER COVER OF THE DENSE SMOKE, THE VALIANT THUNDER GOD STRIKES OUT AGAIN, WITH TELLING EFFECT!

AHH! I *KNEW* THIS WOULD MAKE YOU RELEASE YOUR HOLD ON ME!

THAT WAS QUICK THINKING, LOKI! NOW QUICKLY-- WE MUST FIND THE GOLDEN APPLES AND *FLEE!*

BAH! I DID NOT DO IT TO SAVE *YOU*-- MERELY TO CREATE A DIVERSION FOR *ME!* FOR I *KNOW* WHERE THE APPLES ARE HIDDEN!

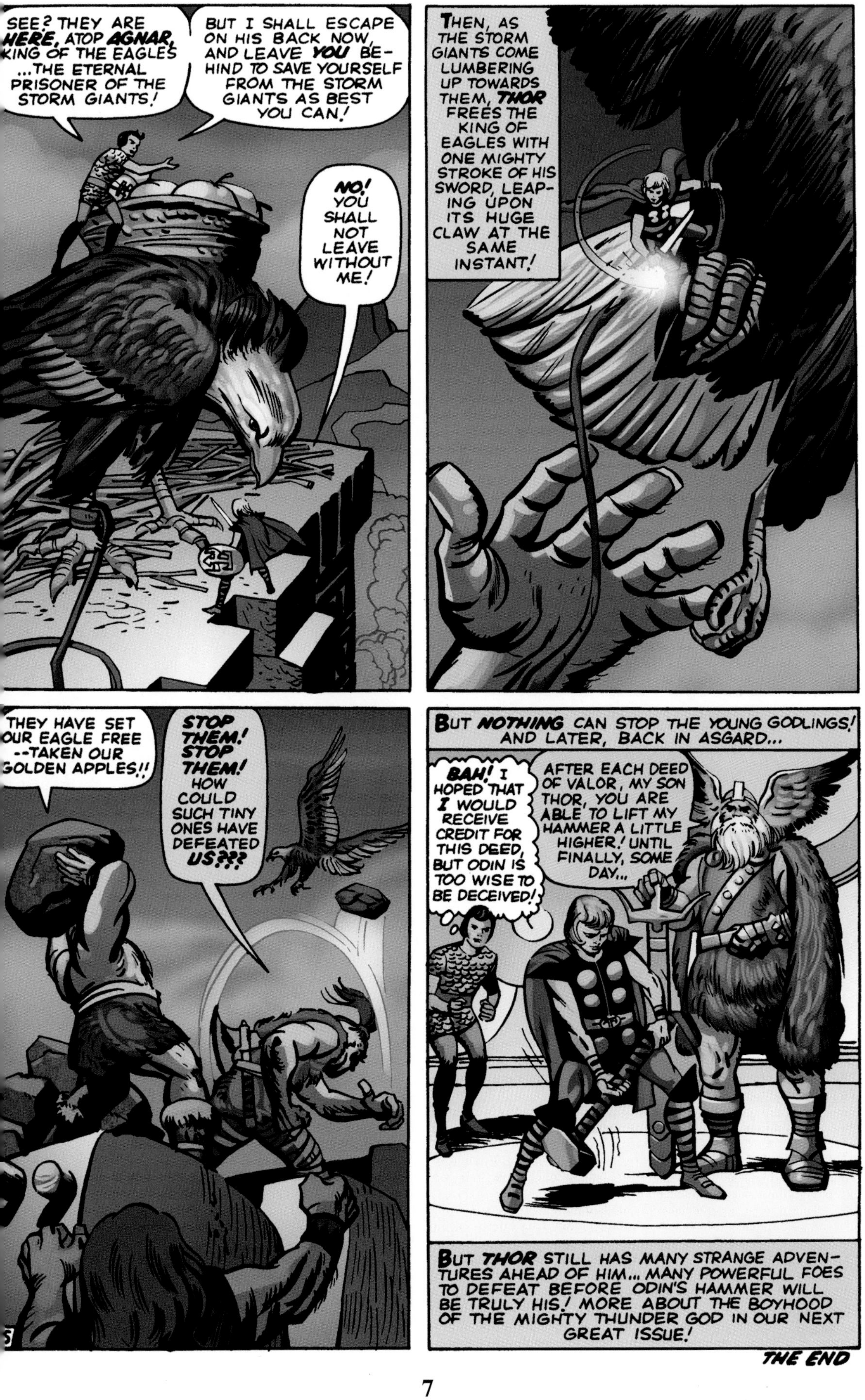
SEE? THEY ARE HERE, ATOP AGNAR, KING OF THE EAGLES ...THE ETERNAL PRISONER OF THE STORM GIANTS!
BUT I SHALL ESCAPE ON HIS BACK NOW, AND LEAVE YOU BEHIND TO SAVE YOURSELF FROM THE STORM GIANTS AS BEST YOU CAN!
NO! YOU SHALL NOT LEAVE WITHOUT ME!
THEN, AS THE STORM GIANTS COME LUMBERING UP TOWARDS THEM, THOR FREES THE KING OF EAGLES WITH ONE MIGHTY STROKE OF HIS SWORD, LEAPING UPON ITS HUGE CLAW AT THE SAME INSTANT!
THEY HAVE SET OUR EAGLE FREE --TAKEN OUR GOLDEN APPLES!!
STOP THEM! STOP THEM! HOW COULD SUCH TINY ONES HAVE DEFEATED US???
BUT NOTHING CAN STOP THE YOUNG GODLINGS! AND LATER, BACK IN ASGARD...
BAH! I HOPED THAT I WOULD RECEIVE CREDIT FOR THIS DEED, BUT ODIN IS TOO WISE TO BE DECEIVED!
AFTER EACH DEED OF VALOR, MY SON THOR, YOU ARE ABLE TO LIFT MY HAMMER A LITTLE HIGHER! UNTIL FINALLY, SOME DAY...
BUT THOR STILL HAS MANY STRANGE ADVENTURES AHEAD OF HIM... MANY POWERFUL FOES TO DEFEAT BEFORE ODIN'S HAMMER WILL BE TRULY HIS! MORE ABOUT THE BOYHOOD OF THE MIGHTY THUNDER GOD IN OUR NEXT GREAT ISSUE!
THE END

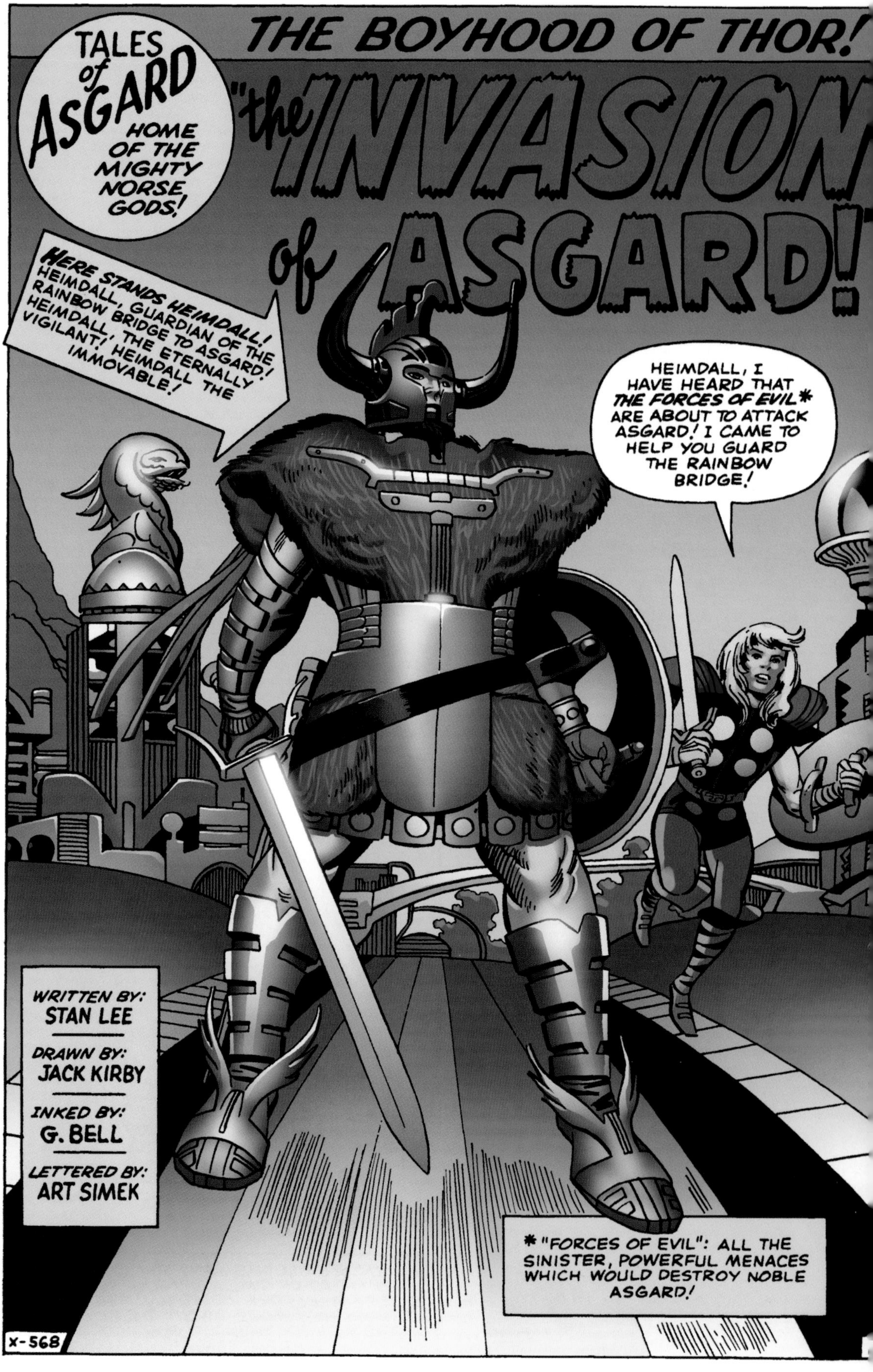
TALES of ASGARD HOME OF THE MIGHTY NORSE GODS!
THE BOYHOOD OF THOR!
"the INVASION of ASGARD!"
HERE STANDS HEIMDALL! HEIMDALL, GUARDIAN OF THE RAINBOW BRIDGE TO ASGARD! HEIMDALL, THE ETERNALLY VIGILANT! HEIMDALL THE IMMOVABLE!
HEIMDALL, I HAVE HEARD THAT THE FORCES OF EVIL* ARE ABOUT TO ATTACK ASGARD! I CAME TO HELP YOU GUARD THE RAINBOW BRIDGE!
WRITTEN BY: STAN LEE
DRAWN BY: JACK KIRBY
INKED BY: G. BELL
LETTERED BY: ART SIMEK
* "FORCES OF EVIL": ALL THE SINISTER, POWERFUL MENACES WHICH WOULD DESTROY NOBLE ASGARD!
X-568

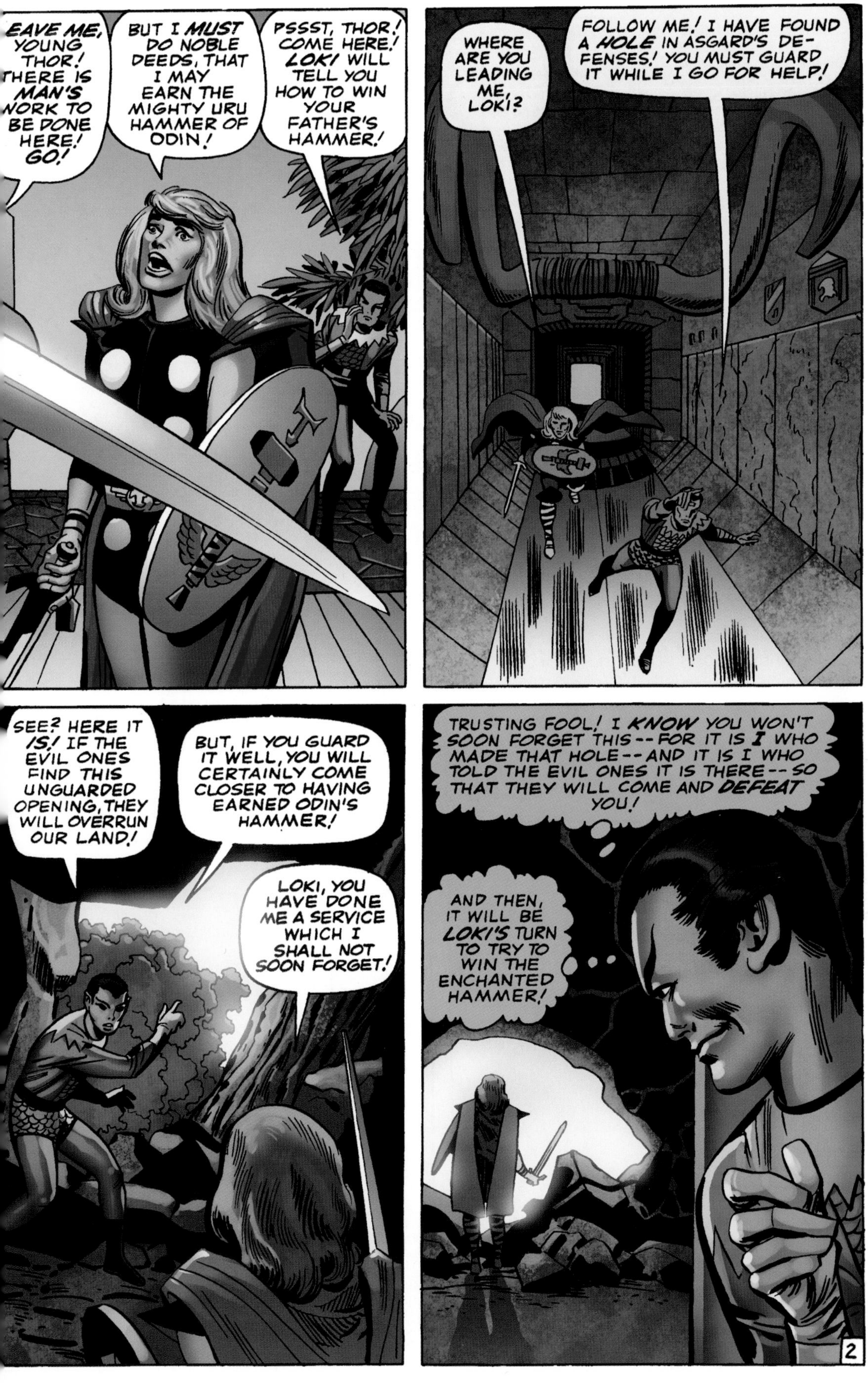
EAVE ME, YOUNG THOR! THERE IS MAN'S WORK TO BE DONE HERE! GO!
BUT I MUST DO NOBLE DEEDS, THAT I MAY EARN THE MIGHTY URU HAMMER OF ODIN!
PSSST, THOR! COME HERE! LOKI WILL TELL YOU HOW TO WIN YOUR FATHER'S HAMMER!
FOLLOW ME! I HAVE FOUND A HOLE IN ASGARD'S DEFENSES! YOU MUST GUARD IT WHILE I GO FOR HELP!
WHERE ARE YOU LEADING ME, LOKI?
SEE? HERE IT IS! IF THE EVIL ONES FIND THIS UNGUARDED OPENING, THEY WILL OVERRUN OUR LAND!
BUT, IF YOU GUARD IT WELL, YOU WILL CERTAINLY COME CLOSER TO HAVING EARNED ODIN'S HAMMER!
LOKI, YOU HAVE DONE ME A SERVICE WHICH I SHALL NOT SOON FORGET!
TRUSTING FOOL! I KNOW YOU WON'T SOON FORGET THIS--FOR IT IS I WHO MADE THAT HOLE--AND IT IS I WHO TOLD THE EVIL ONES IT IS THERE--SO THAT THEY WILL COME AND DEFEAT YOU!
AND THEN, IT WILL BE LOKI'S TURN TO TRY TO WIN THE ENCHANTED HAMMER!
2

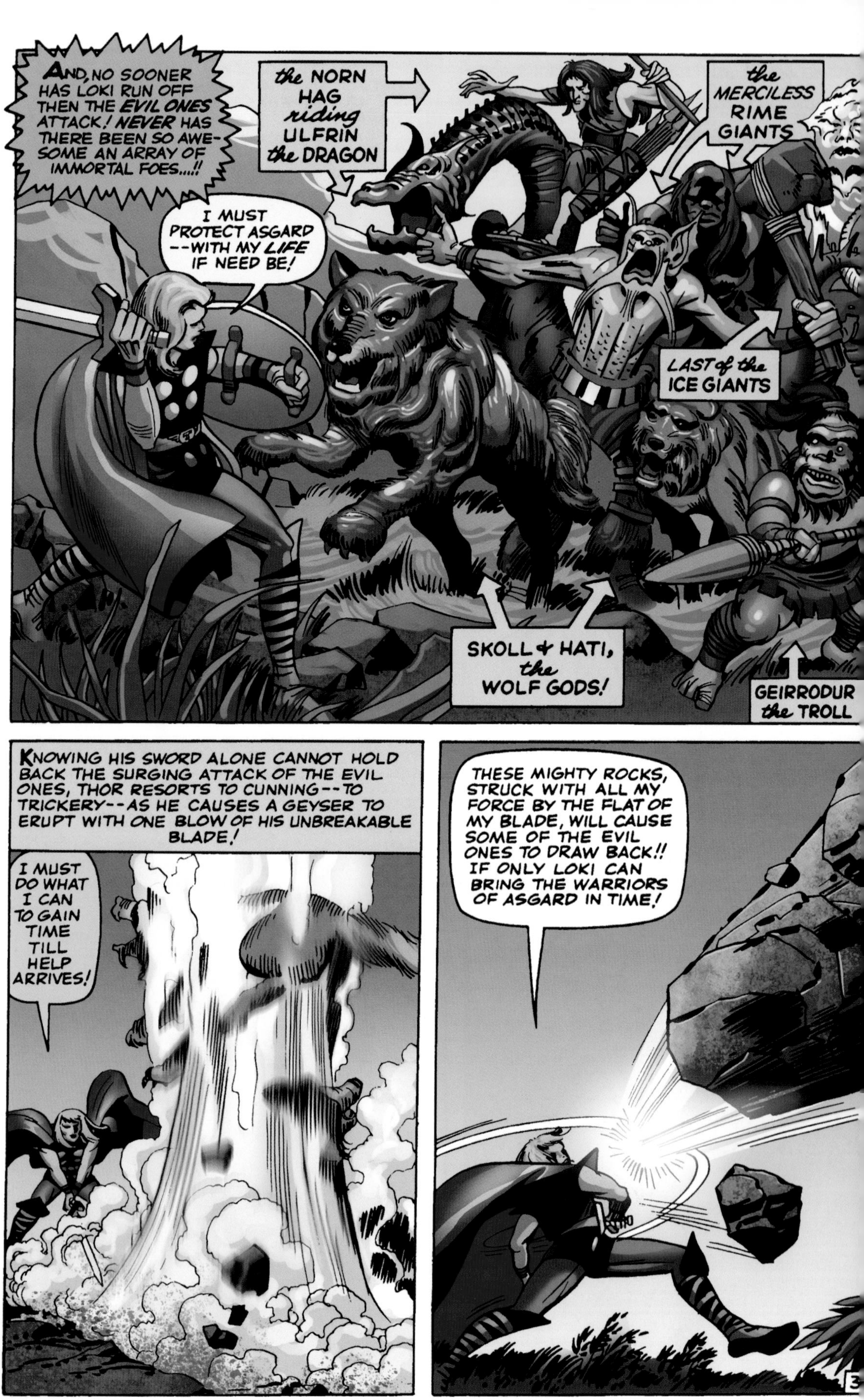

AND, NO SOONER HAS LOKI RUN OFF THEN THE EVIL ONES ATTACK! NEVER HAS THERE BEEN SO AWE-SOME AN ARRAY OF IMMORTAL FOES...!!
the NORN HAG riding ULFRIN the DRAGON
the MERCILESS RIME GIANTS
I MUST PROTECT ASGARD --WITH MY LIFE IF NEED BE!
LAST of the ICE GIANTS
SKOLL & HATI, the WOLF GODS!
GEIRRODUR the TROLL
KNOWING HIS SWORD ALONE CANNOT HOLD BACK THE SURGING ATTACK OF THE EVIL ONES, THOR RESORTS TO CUNNING--TO TRICKERY--AS HE CAUSES A GEYSER TO ERUPT WITH ONE BLOW OF HIS UNBREAKABLE BLADE!
I MUST DO WHAT I CAN TO GAIN TIME TILL HELP ARRIVES!
THESE MIGHTY ROCKS, STRUCK WITH ALL MY FORCE BY THE FLAT OF MY BLADE, WILL CAUSE SOME OF THE EVIL ONES TO DRAW BACK!! IF ONLY LOKI CAN BRING THE WARRIORS OF ASGARD IN TIME!
3

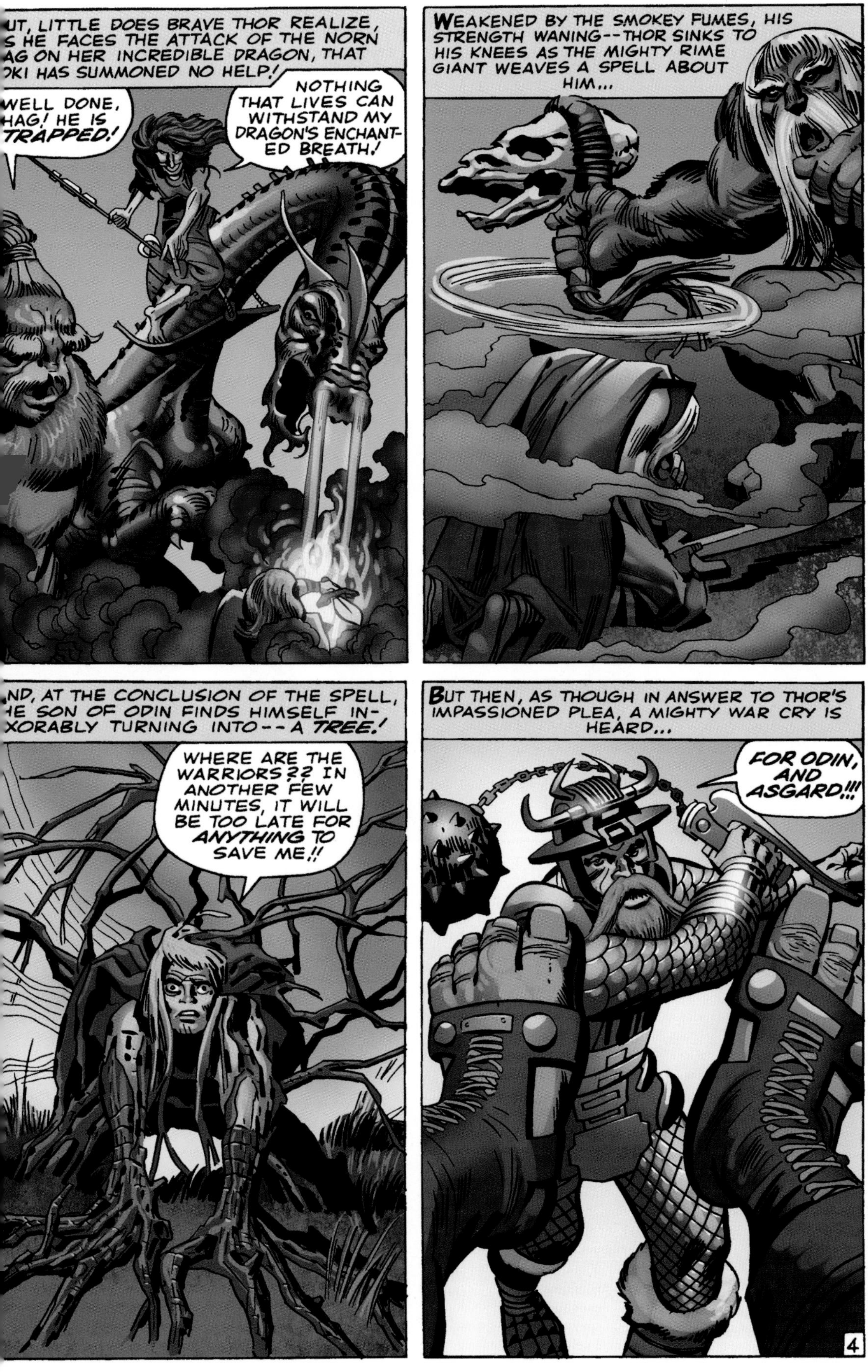
UT, LITTLE DOES BRAVE THOR REALIZE, S HE FACES THE ATTACK OF THE NORN AG ON HER INCREDIBLE DRAGON, THAT OKI HAS SUMMONED NO HELP!
WELL DONE, HAG! HE IS TRAPPED!
NOTHING THAT LIVES CAN WITHSTAND MY DRAGON'S ENCHANTED BREATH!
WEAKENED BY THE SMOKEY FUMES, HIS STRENGTH WANING--THOR SINKS TO HIS KNEES AS THE MIGHTY RIME GIANT WEAVES A SPELL ABOUT HIM...
ND, AT THE CONCLUSION OF THE SPELL, HE SON OF ODIN FINDS HIMSELF INXORABLY TURNING INTO--A TREE!
WHERE ARE THE WARRIORS?? IN ANOTHER FEW MINUTES, IT WILL BE TOO LATE FOR ANYTHING TO SAVE ME!!
BUT THEN, AS THOUGH IN ANSWER TO THOR'S IMPASSIONED PLEA, A MIGHTY WAR CRY IS HEARD...
FOR ODIN, AND ASGARD!!!
4

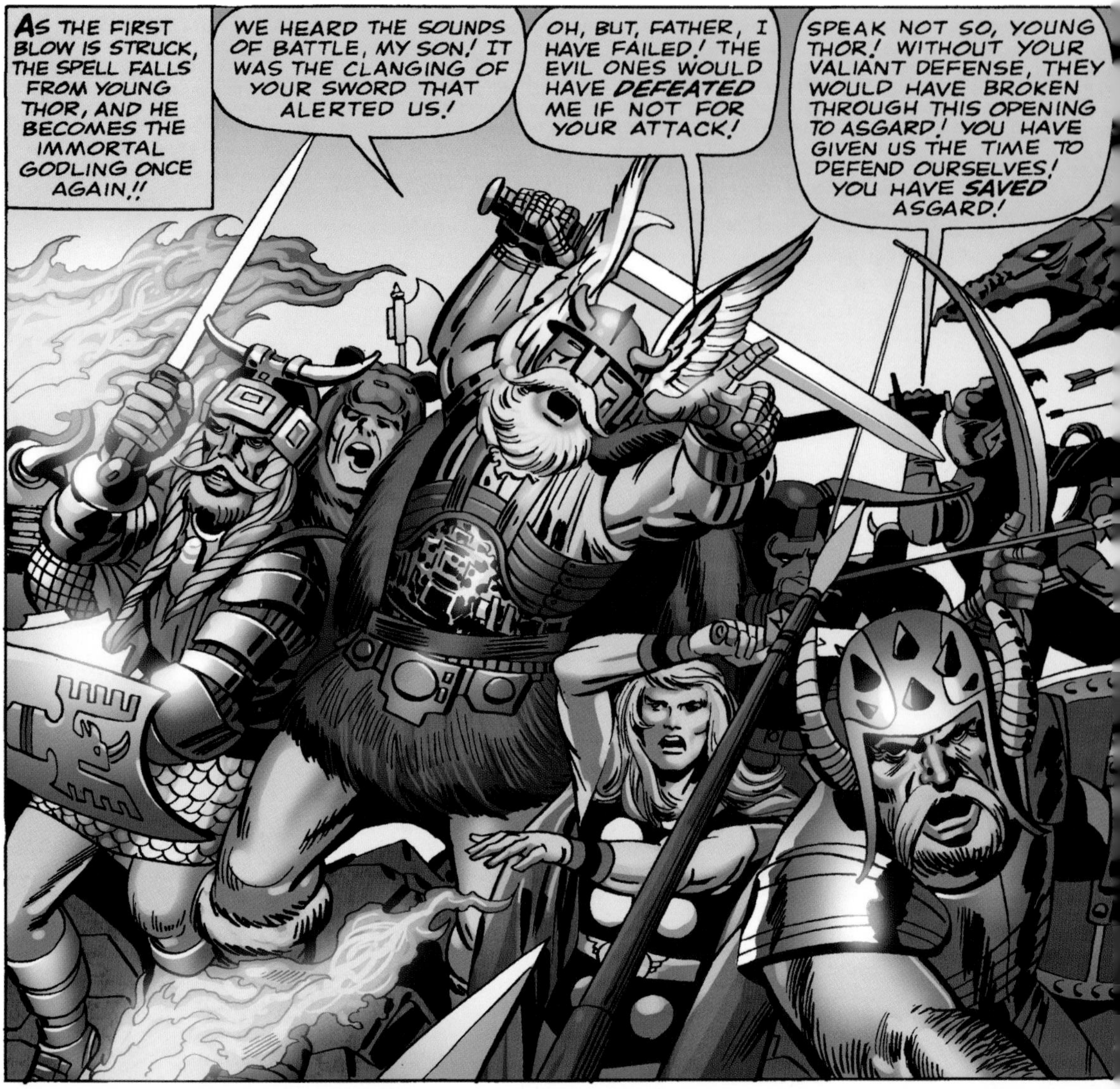

AS THE FIRST BLOW IS STRUCK, THE SPELL FALLS FROM YOUNG THOR, AND HE BECOMES THE IMMORTAL GODLING ONCE AGAIN!!
WE HEARD THE SOUNDS OF BATTLE, MY SON! IT WAS THE CLANGING OF YOUR SWORD THAT ALERTED US!
OH, BUT, FATHER, I HAVE FAILED! THE EVIL ONES WOULD HAVE ***DEFEATED*** ME IF NOT FOR YOUR ATTACK!
SPEAK NOT SO, YOUNG THOR! WITHOUT YOUR VALIANT DEFENSE, THEY WOULD HAVE BROKEN THROUGH THIS OPENING TO ASGARD! YOU HAVE GIVEN US THE TIME TO DEFEND OURSELVES! YOU HAVE ***SAVED*** ASGARD!

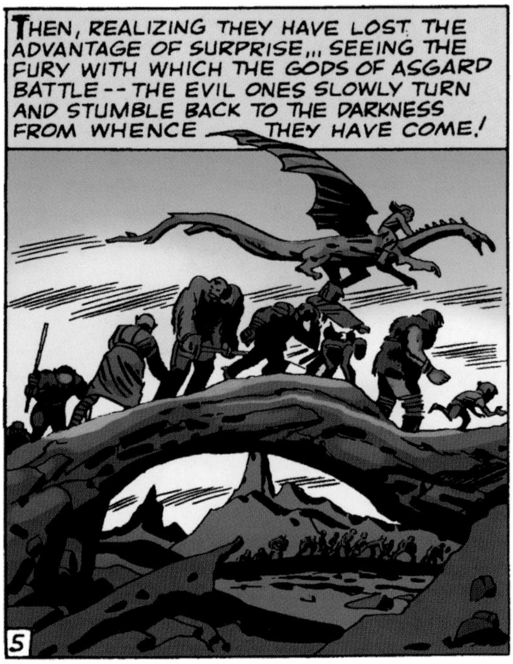

THEN, REALIZING THEY HAVE LOST THE ADVANTAGE OF SURPRISE... SEEING THE FURY WITH WHICH THE GODS OF ASGARD BATTLE -- THE EVIL ONES SLOWLY TURN AND STUMBLE BACK TO THE DARKNESS FROM WHENCE THEY HAVE COME!
5

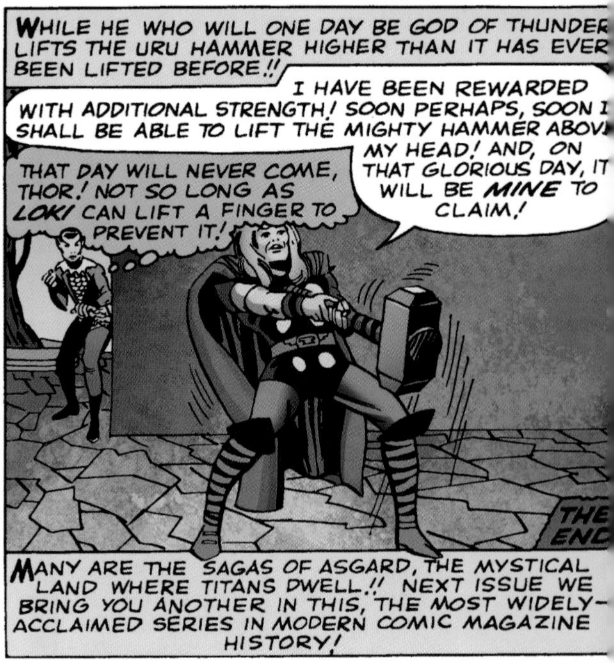

WHILE HE WHO WILL ONE DAY BE GOD OF THUNDER LIFTS THE URU HAMMER HIGHER THAN IT HAS EVER BEEN LIFTED BEFORE!!
I HAVE BEEN REWARDED WITH ADDITIONAL STRENGTH! SOON PERHAPS, SOON I SHALL BE ABLE TO LIFT THE MIGHTY HAMMER ABOV MY HEAD! AND, ON THAT GLORIOUS DAY, IT WILL BE ***MINE*** TO CLAIM!
THAT DAY WILL NEVER COME, THOR! NOT SO LONG AS ***LOKI*** CAN LIFT A FINGER TO PREVENT IT!
THE END
MANY ARE THE SAGAS OF ASGARD, THE MYSTICAL LAND WHERE TITANS DWELL!! NEXT ISSUE WE BRING YOU ANOTHER IN THIS, THE MOST WIDELY-ACCLAIMED SERIES IN MODERN COMIC MAGAZINE HISTORY!

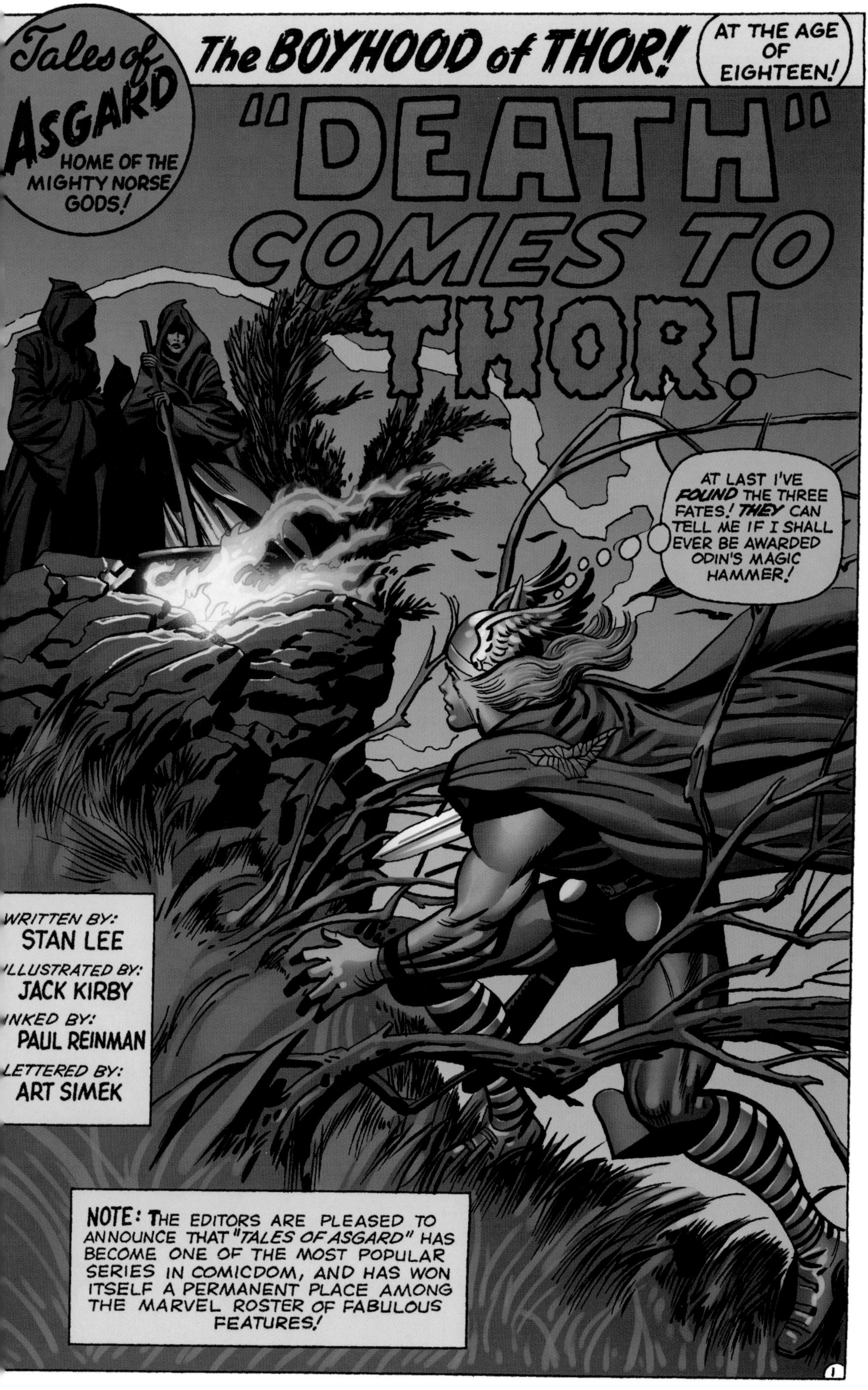
Tales of ASGARD
HOME OF THE MIGHTY NORSE GODS!
The BOYHOOD of THOR!
AT THE AGE OF EIGHTEEN!
"DEATH" COMES TO THOR!
AT LAST I'VE FOUND THE THREE FATES! THEY CAN TELL ME IF I SHALL EVER BE AWARDED ODIN'S MAGIC HAMMER!
WRITTEN BY: STAN LEE
ILLUSTRATED BY: JACK KIRBY
INKED BY: PAUL REINMAN
LETTERED BY: ART SIMEK
NOTE: THE EDITORS ARE PLEASED TO ANNOUNCE THAT "TALES OF ASGARD" HAS BECOME ONE OF THE MOST POPULAR SERIES IN COMICDOM, AND HAS WON ITSELF A PERMANENT PLACE AMONG THE MARVEL ROSTER OF FABULOUS FEATURES!
1

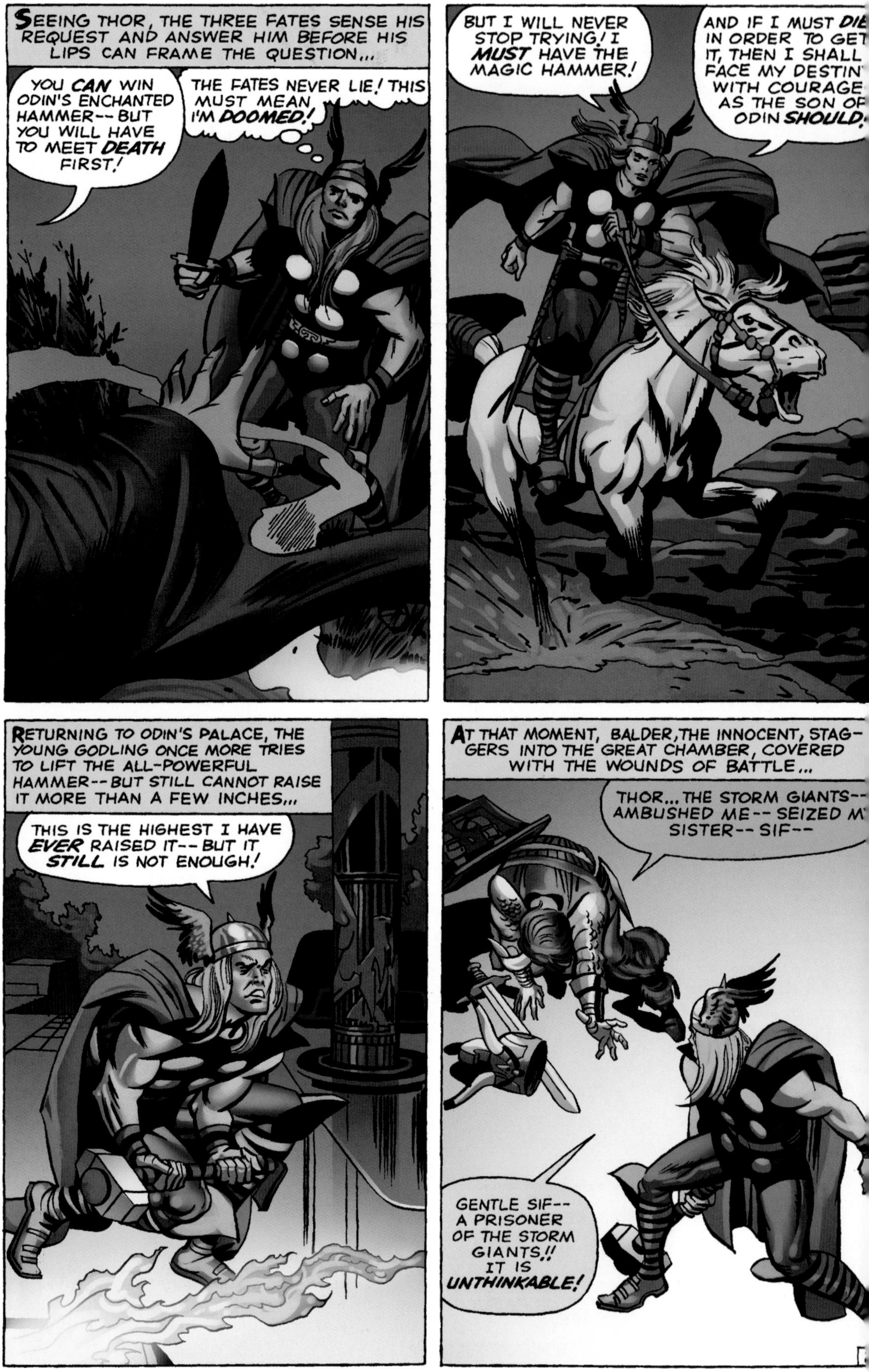
SEEING THOR, THE THREE FATES SENSE HIS REQUEST AND ANSWER HIM BEFORE HIS LIPS CAN FRAME THE QUESTION...
YOU CAN WIN ODIN'S ENCHANTED HAMMER-- BUT YOU WILL HAVE TO MEET DEATH FIRST!
THE FATES NEVER LIE! THIS MUST MEAN I'M DOOMED!
BUT I WILL NEVER STOP TRYING! I MUST HAVE THE MAGIC HAMMER!
AND IF I MUST DI IN ORDER TO GET IT, THEN I SHALL FACE MY DESTIN WITH COURAGE AS THE SON OF ODIN SHOULD!
RETURNING TO ODIN'S PALACE, THE YOUNG GODLING ONCE MORE TRIES TO LIFT THE ALL-POWERFUL HAMMER--BUT STILL CANNOT RAISE IT MORE THAN A FEW INCHES...
THIS IS THE HIGHEST I HAVE EVER RAISED IT-- BUT IT STILL IS NOT ENOUGH!
AT THAT MOMENT, BALDER, THE INNOCENT, STAGGERS INTO THE GREAT CHAMBER, COVERED WITH THE WOUNDS OF BATTLE...
THOR... THE STORM GIANTS-- AMBUSHED ME-- SEIZED M SISTER-- SIF--
GENTLE SIF-- A PRISONER OF THE STORM GIANTS!! IT IS UNTHINKABLE!

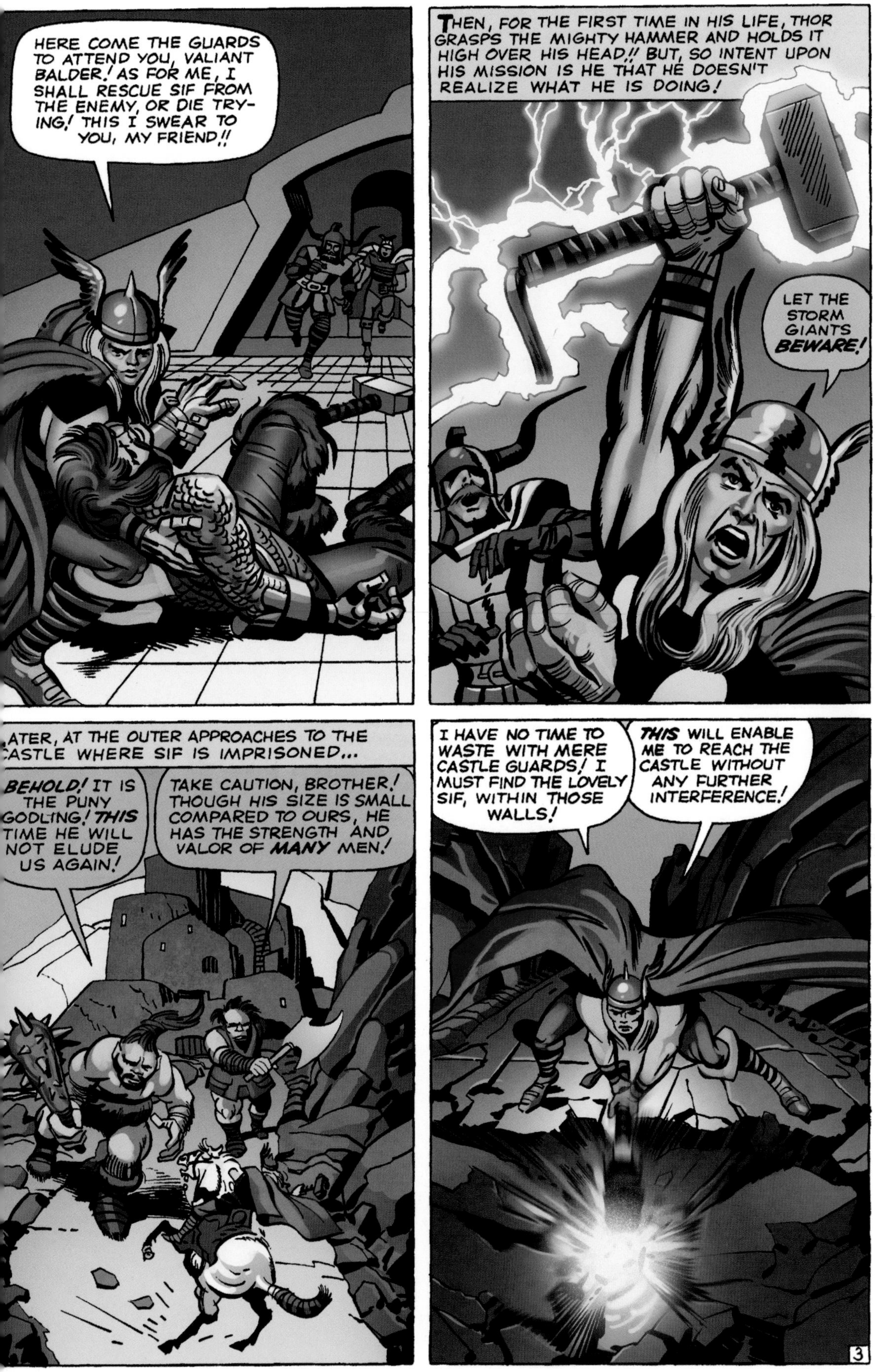
HERE COME THE GUARDS TO ATTEND YOU, VALIANT BALDER! AS FOR ME, I SHALL RESCUE SIF FROM THE ENEMY, OR DIE TRYING! THIS I SWEAR TO YOU, MY FRIEND!!
THEN, FOR THE FIRST TIME IN HIS LIFE, THOR GRASPS THE MIGHTY HAMMER AND HOLDS IT HIGH OVER HIS HEAD!! BUT, SO INTENT UPON HIS MISSION IS HE THAT HE DOESN'T REALIZE WHAT HE IS DOING!
LET THE STORM GIANTS BEWARE!
ATER, AT THE OUTER APPROACHES TO THE CASTLE WHERE SIF IS IMPRISONED...
BEHOLD! IT IS THE PUNY GODLING! THIS TIME HE WILL NOT ELUDE US AGAIN!
TAKE CAUTION, BROTHER! THOUGH HIS SIZE IS SMALL COMPARED TO OURS, HE HAS THE STRENGTH AND VALOR OF MANY MEN!
I HAVE NO TIME TO WASTE WITH MERE CASTLE GUARDS! I MUST FIND THE LOVELY SIF, WITHIN THOSE WALLS!
THIS WILL ENABLE ME TO REACH THE CASTLE WITHOUT ANY FURTHER INTERFERENCE!
3

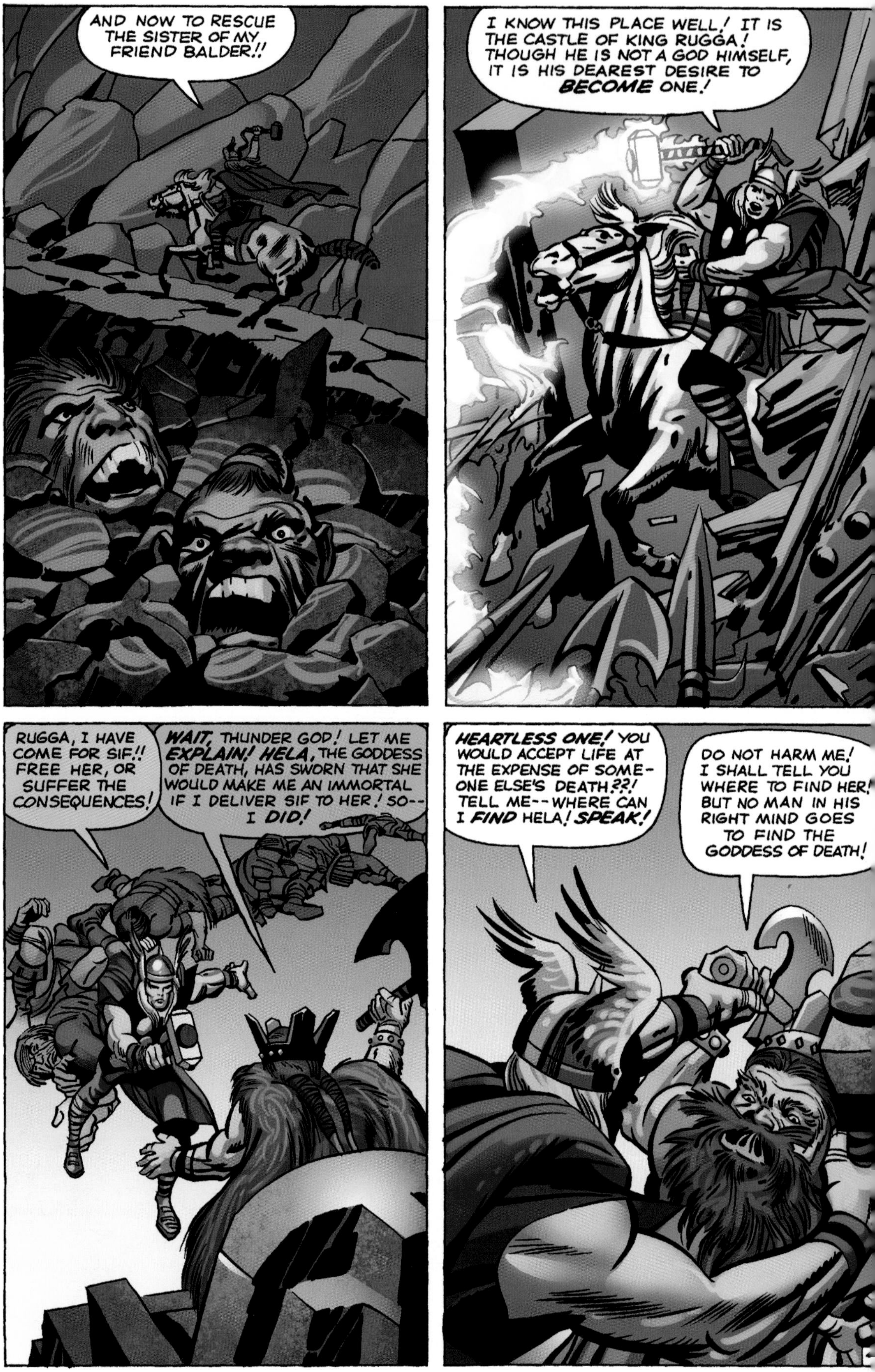
AND NOW TO RESCUE THE SISTER OF MY FRIEND BALDER!!
I KNOW THIS PLACE WELL! IT IS THE CASTLE OF KING RUGGA! THOUGH HE IS NOT A GOD HIMSELF, IT IS HIS DEAREST DESIRE TO BECOME ONE!
RUGGA, I HAVE COME FOR SIF!! FREE HER, OR SUFFER THE CONSEQUENCES!
WAIT, THUNDER GOD! LET ME EXPLAIN! HELA, THE GODDESS OF DEATH, HAS SWORN THAT SHE WOULD MAKE ME AN IMMORTAL IF I DELIVER SIF TO HER! SO-- I DID!
HEARTLESS ONE! YOU WOULD ACCEPT LIFE AT THE EXPENSE OF SOME-ONE ELSE'S DEATH??! TELL ME--WHERE CAN I FIND HELA! SPEAK!
DO NOT HARM ME! I SHALL TELL YOU WHERE TO FIND HER! BUT NO MAN IN HIS RIGHT MIND GOES TO FIND THE GODDESS OF DEATH!

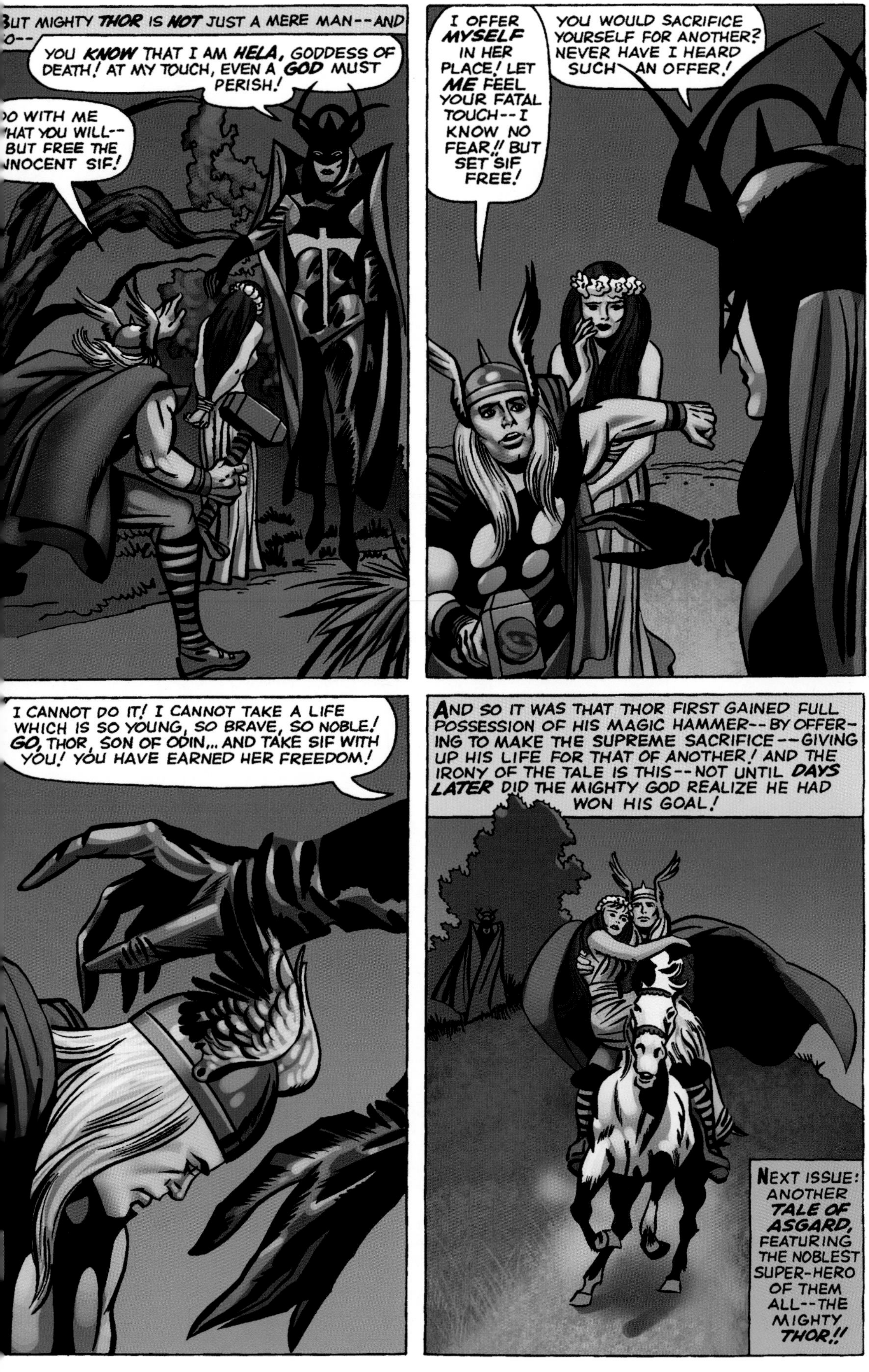
BUT MIGHTY THOR IS NOT JUST A MERE MAN--AND SO--
YOU KNOW THAT I AM HELA, GODDESS OF DEATH! AT MY TOUCH, EVEN A GOD MUST PERISH!
DO WITH ME WHAT YOU WILL--BUT FREE THE INNOCENT SIF!
I OFFER MYSELF IN HER PLACE! LET ME FEEL YOUR FATAL TOUCH--I KNOW NO FEAR!! BUT SET SIF FREE!
YOU WOULD SACRIFICE YOURSELF FOR ANOTHER? NEVER HAVE I HEARD SUCH AN OFFER!
I CANNOT DO IT! I CANNOT TAKE A LIFE WHICH IS SO YOUNG, SO BRAVE, SO NOBLE! GO, THOR, SON OF ODIN... AND TAKE SIF WITH YOU! YOU HAVE EARNED HER FREEDOM!
AND SO IT WAS THAT THOR FIRST GAINED FULL POSSESSION OF HIS MAGIC HAMMER--BY OFFERING TO MAKE THE SUPREME SACRIFICE--GIVING UP HIS LIFE FOR THAT OF ANOTHER! AND THE IRONY OF THE TALE IS THIS--NOT UNTIL DAYS LATER DID THE MIGHTY GOD REALIZE HE HAD WON HIS GOAL!
NEXT ISSUE: ANOTHER TALE OF ASGARD, FEATURING THE NOBLEST SUPER-HERO OF THEM ALL--THE MIGHTY THOR!!

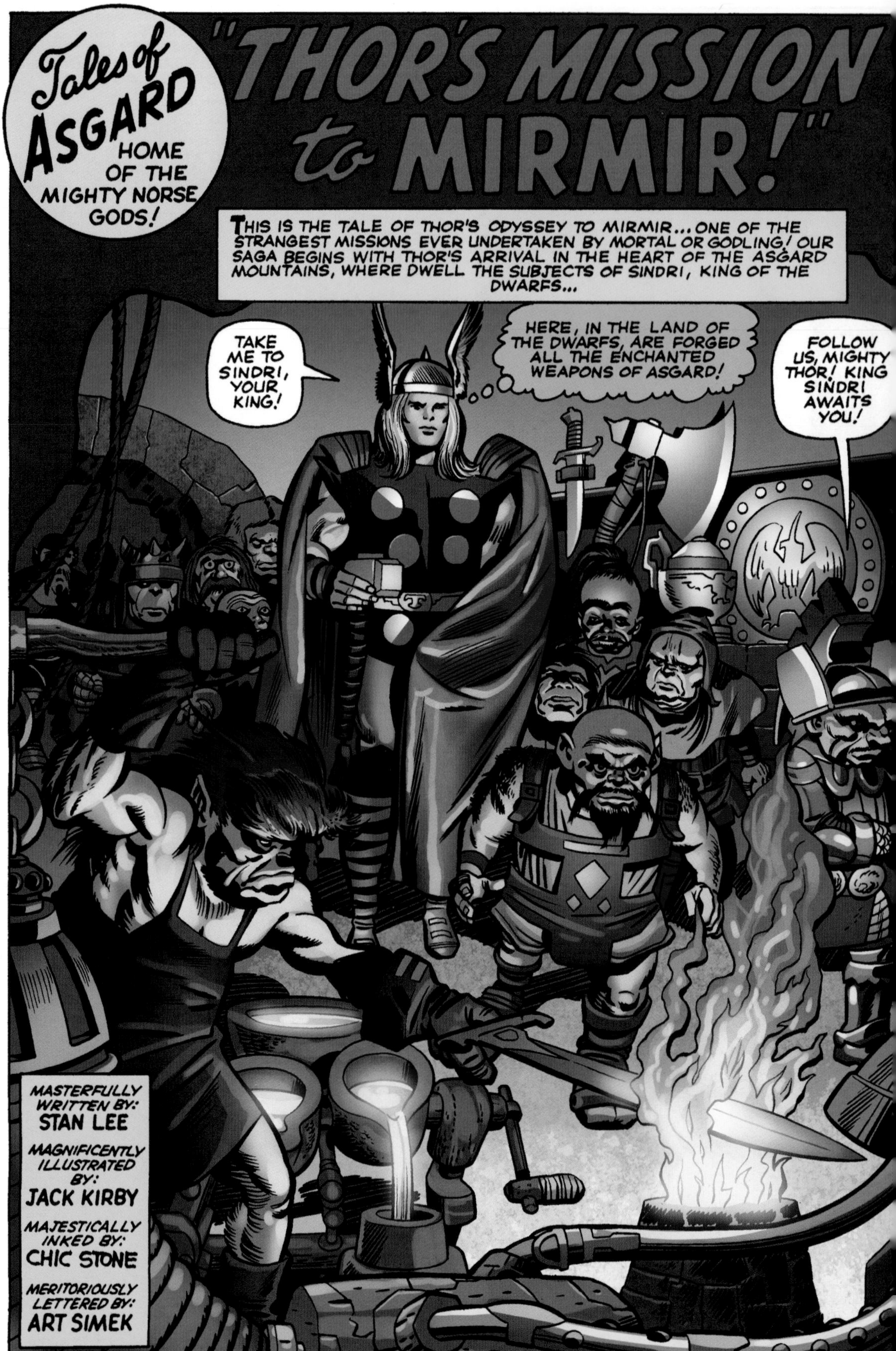

Tales of ASGARD HOME OF THE MIGHTY NORSE GODS!
"THOR'S MISSION to MIRMIR!"
THIS IS THE TALE OF THOR'S ODYSSEY TO MIRMIR... ONE OF THE STRANGEST MISSIONS EVER UNDERTAKEN BY MORTAL OR GODLING! OUR SAGA BEGINS WITH THOR'S ARRIVAL IN THE HEART OF THE ASGARD MOUNTAINS, WHERE DWELL THE SUBJECTS OF SINDRI, KING OF THE DWARFS...
TAKE ME TO SINDRI, YOUR KING!
HERE, IN THE LAND OF THE DWARFS, ARE FORGED ALL THE ENCHANTED WEAPONS OF ASGARD!
FOLLOW US, MIGHTY THOR! KING SINDRI AWAITS YOU!
MASTERFULLY WRITTEN BY: STAN LEE
MAGNIFICENTLY ILLUSTRATED BY: JACK KIRBY
MAJESTICALLY INKED BY: CHIC STONE
METICULOUSLY LETTERED BY: ART SIMEK
X-625

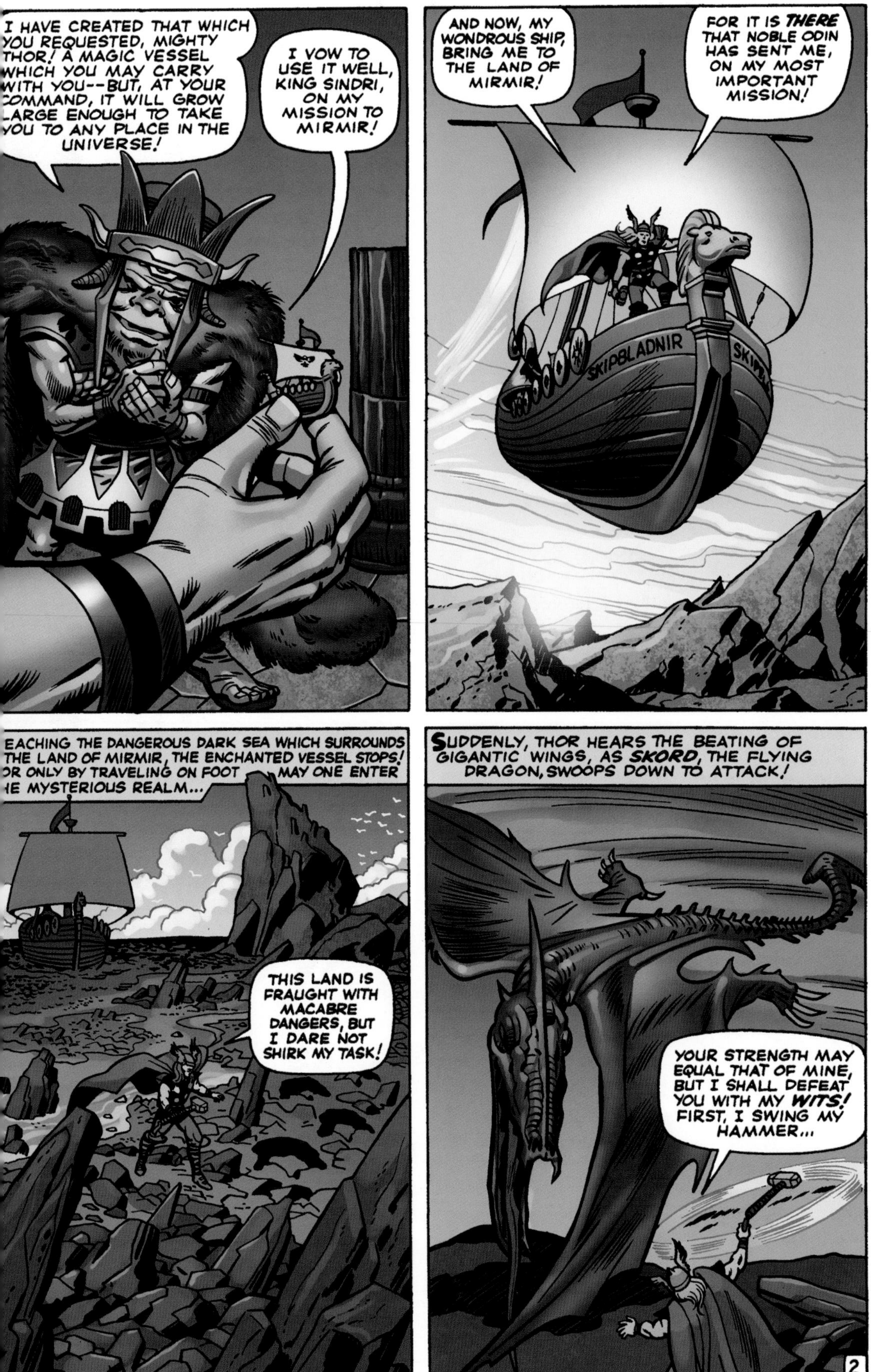
I HAVE CREATED THAT WHICH YOU REQUESTED, MIGHTY THOR! A MAGIC VESSEL WHICH YOU MAY CARRY WITH YOU--BUT, AT YOUR COMMAND, IT WILL GROW LARGE ENOUGH TO TAKE YOU TO ANY PLACE IN THE UNIVERSE!
I VOW TO USE IT WELL, KING SINDRI, ON MY MISSION TO MIRMIR!
AND NOW, MY WONDROUS SHIP, BRING ME TO THE LAND OF MIRMIR!
FOR IT IS THERE THAT NOBLE ODIN HAS SENT ME, ON MY MOST IMPORTANT MISSION!
SKIPBLADNIR
EACHING THE DANGEROUS DARK SEA WHICH SURROUNDS THE LAND OF MIRMIR, THE ENCHANTED VESSEL STOPS! OR ONLY BY TRAVELING ON FOOT MAY ONE ENTER IE MYSTERIOUS REALM...
THIS LAND IS FRAUGHT WITH MACABRE DANGERS, BUT I DARE NOT SHIRK MY TASK!
SUDDENLY, THOR HEARS THE BEATING OF GIGANTIC WINGS, AS SKORD, THE FLYING DRAGON, SWOOPS DOWN TO ATTACK!
YOUR STRENGTH MAY EQUAL THAT OF MINE, BUT I SHALL DEFEAT YOU WITH MY WITS! FIRST, I SWING MY HAMMER...
2

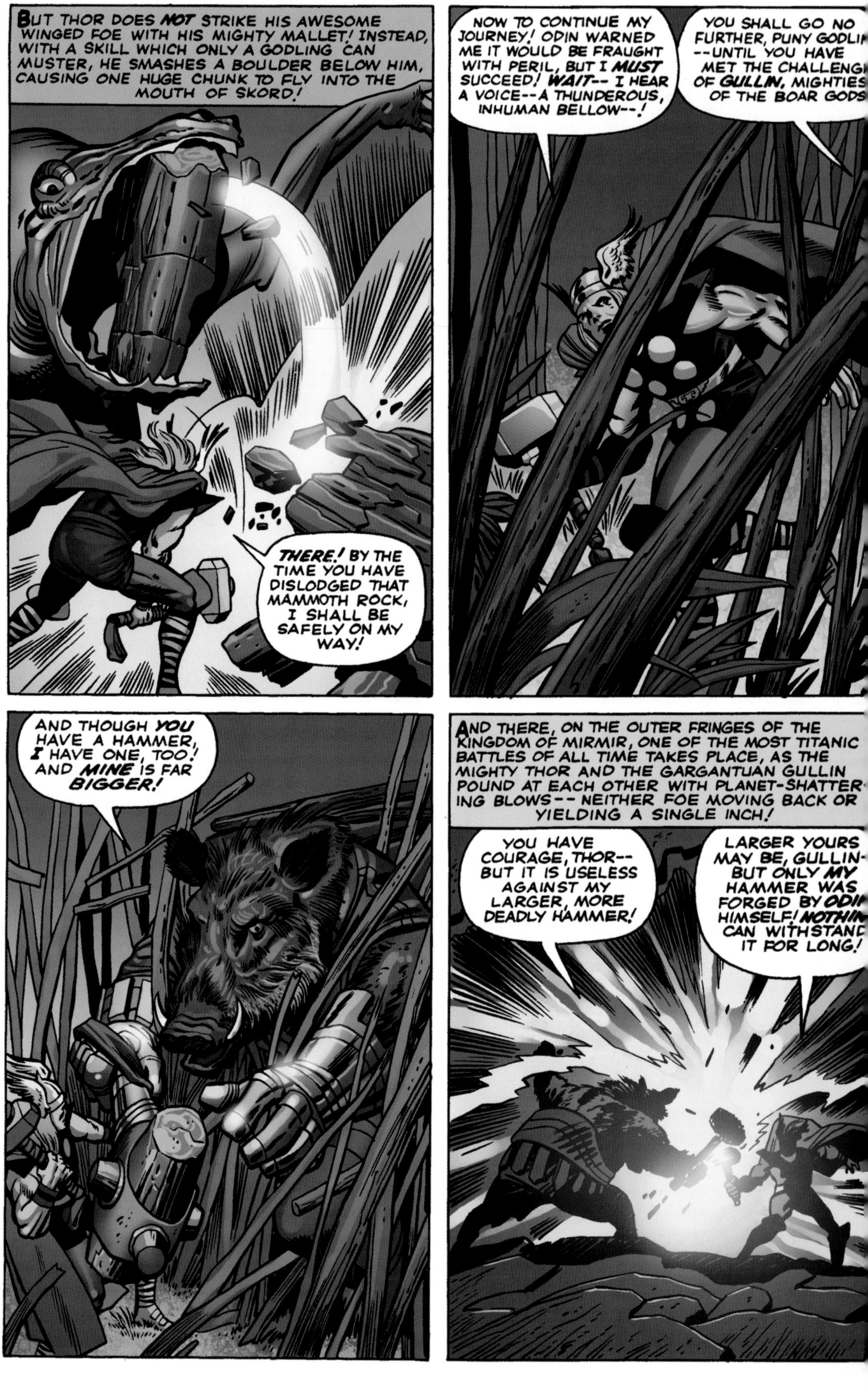
BUT THOR DOES NOT STRIKE HIS AWESOME WINGED FOE WITH HIS MIGHTY MALLET! INSTEAD, WITH A SKILL WHICH ONLY A GODLING CAN MUSTER, HE SMASHES A BOULDER BELOW HIM, CAUSING ONE HUGE CHUNK TO FLY INTO THE MOUTH OF SKORD!
THERE! BY THE TIME YOU HAVE DISLODGED THAT MAMMOTH ROCK, I SHALL BE SAFELY ON MY WAY!
NOW TO CONTINUE MY JOURNEY! ODIN WARNED ME IT WOULD BE FRAUGHT WITH PERIL, BUT I MUST SUCCEED! WAIT-- I HEAR A VOICE--A THUNDEROUS, INHUMAN BELLOW--!
YOU SHALL GO NO FURTHER, PUNY GODLI --UNTIL YOU HAVE MET THE CHALLENG OF GULLIN, MIGHTIES OF THE BOAR GODS
AND THOUGH YOU HAVE A HAMMER, I HAVE ONE, TOO! AND MINE IS FAR BIGGER!
AND THERE, ON THE OUTER FRINGES OF THE KINGDOM OF MIRMIR, ONE OF THE MOST TITANIC BATTLES OF ALL TIME TAKES PLACE, AS THE MIGHTY THOR AND THE GARGANTUAN GULLIN POUND AT EACH OTHER WITH PLANET-SHATTERING BLOWS-- NEITHER FOE MOVING BACK OR YIELDING A SINGLE INCH!
YOU HAVE COURAGE, THOR-- BUT IT IS USELESS AGAINST MY LARGER, MORE DEADLY HAMMER!
LARGER YOURS MAY BE, GULLIN-BUT ONLY MY HAMMER WAS FORGED BY ODI HIMSELF! NOTHIN CAN WITHSTAND IT FOR LONG!

AND THE NEXT TREMENDOUS IMPACT DEMON-STRATES THE *TRUTH* OF MIGHTY THOR'S WORDS, AS GULLIN'S WEAPON IS SHATTERED TO BITS BEFORE HIS VERY EYES!

NOW YOU ARE *DEFENSELESS*, GULLIN! I ORDER YOU TO FLEE BEFORE MY HAMMER STRIKES AGAIN!

HE HAD NO CHOICE BUT TO ALLOW ME FREE PASSAGE! AND NOW, MY GOAL IS ALMOST AT HAND...

I MUST FOLLOW THIS MAIN STREAM WHICH WILL LEAD ME DIRECTLY TO KING MIRMIR HIMSELF!!

AND FINALLY, AT THE HEAD OF THE STREAM, BEHIND THE MYSTIC FOUNTAIN WHICH FEEDS ALL THE WORLD'S OCEANS, THOR FINDS THE ONE HE SEEKS!

THOR! IT IS *YOU*! DOES THAT MEAN MY MOMENT IS AT HAND?

YES! NOBLE ODIN HAS SENT YOU THIS MESSAGE --YOU MUST DO WHAT YOU ARE PLEDGED TO DO!

ODIN HAS SENT THIS BRANCH, FROM YGGDRASILL, THE TREE OF LIFE! YOU KNOW WHAT MUST BE DONE!

SO BE IT! MIRMIR WILL BE TRUE TO HIS SACRED TRUST! GIVE ME THE MAGIC BRANCH!

4

I PLACE THE BRANCH OF LIFE INTO THE ENCHANTED FOUNTAIN, AND SLOWLY STIR THE MYSTIC WATERS! NOW LET THEM SPILL INTO THE WORLD BELOW...

AND, FAR BELOW, IN THE PLACE CALLED *MIDGARD,* SOME OF THE MAGIC DROPS TRICKLE ONTO A PAIR OF TREES, AN ALDER AND AN ASH, PLANTED AGES BEFORE BY WISE ODIN...

...AND LO, THE TREES SLOWLY CHANGE FORM UNTIL... WHERE STOOD AN ALDER AND AN ASH, WE NOW SEE THE PROUD FIGURES OF *ASKE* AND *EMBLA,* DESTINED TO START A NEW RACE, IN THE IMAGE OF THE IMMORTALS OF ASGARD!

5

THUS, HIS MISSION ACCOMPLISHED, THE MIGHTY THOR RETURNS TO HIS HOME IN ASGARD, TO AWAIT THE NEWER AND MORE STARTLING TASKS WHICH ODIN HAS IN STORE!

THE END

EDITOR'S NOTE: FREELY TRANSLATED, THE TALE YOU HAVE JUST READ IS PART OF THE 'NORSE LEGENDS WHICH DEAL WITH THE BIRTH OF MAN KIND AND THE DAYS BEFORE THE BEGINNING OF TIME!'

ASGARD

Asgard is a small otherdimensional planetary body (its surface area being about the same as that of the continental United States), whose nature and physics are different from those of planetary bodies in the Earthly dimension. Asgard is not a sphere like the Earth or Moon, but a relatively flat asteroid-like landmass suspended in space. Asgard does not rotate about its axis, nor does it revolve around a sun. Asgard has intervals of night and day (of undisclosed durations) even though it does not rotate. There is no evidence of changing seasons, however. It is not known if Asgard's source of light and heat is the Earth's sun, a sun in the Asgardian dimension whose gravity does not exert itself on Asgard, or a glowing ball of light dissimilar to a star in most of its properties. Unlike Earth, where the force of gravitation radiates from the center of the sphere, Asgard's gravity apparently radiates from some point or object beneath the suspended landmass. Consequently, there is a top side to Asgard, upon which beings can stand, and a bottom side where beings cannot stand and from which they will fall through space toward the source of gravitation. At the boundaries of Asgard's landmass, a being or object can step off into the void.

There is apparently some force that keeps the bottom and edges of Asgard's landmass from eroding away. Whatever this force is also prevents the bodies of water which are at certain of Asgard's boundaries from pouring off into the void, as well as preventing Asgard's atmosphere from escaping. Asgard has been described as floating on a "Sea of Space." This sea apparently has a surface, one that is navigable by certain Asgardian ships that resemble Viking longboats. The exact nature of space in the Asgardian dimension is unknown.

While the gravity of Asgard is roughly analogous to Earth's, common matter is considerably denser on an average. Consequently a chair made of Asgardian wood would be more massive (and heavier) than a chair made of analagous Earthly wood. Rocks, water, flesh, bone, steel — all matter is denser and thus more durable.

Besides all of the anomalies described above, Asgard is connected in some as yet unknown way with at least two other dimensional planes, one of which is that of the Earth (whom the Asgardians call *Midgard*, a word meaning "Middle Realm"). The Asgardians refer to all of the major known inhabited realms of their cosmology as the "Nine Worlds." Only four of the Nine Worlds are located on the main Asgardian landmass: *Asgard*, home of the Gods, *Vanaheim*, home of the Asgardians' sister race, the Vanir, *Nidavellir*, home of the Dwarves, and *Alfheim*, home of the Light Elves.

The remainder of the Nine Worlds are on separate landmasses isolated from one another by interdimensional space. (For the sake of creating a comprehensible diagram, the Nine Worlds of Asgard are placed in a multi-leveled configuration. These levels do not represent any real physical distances or relationships. Instead, they represent the interdimensional relationships between the realms.) *Midgard*, our Earth, does not appear to be physically affected by the motions of any of the other physical bodies in the Asgardian cosmology, although Earth's axis (the imaginary pole around which it rotates) is in alignment with one of the roots of Yggdrasil, the cosmic ash tree that stands in Asgard. *Jotunheim*, the world of the giants, is a flat ring-shaped realm with high mountains along its inner edge. It is apparently on its own separate dimension plane, discrete from Asgard's and Earth's. *Svartalfheim*, home of the Dark Elves, is another asteroid-like landmass, smaller than Asgard. There are numerous nexus-portals between the mountains of Jotunheim and Svartalfheim and the mountains of Asgard permitting easy passage by denizens of each realm. These passageways make Jotunheim and Svartalfheim seem like "underworlds" of the Asgardian continent itself.

The eighth of the Nine Worlds is *Hel*, realm of the dead, and its sister realm, *Niffleheim*. In the Asgardian scheme of afterlife, the heroes and honored dead go to Valhalla, a special region of Asgard, the common dead go to Hel, and the dishonored dead (murderers and other evildoers) go to Niffleheim. Hel, Niffleheim, and Valhalla possess the necessary physical conditions to permit the astral forms of the deceased to exist there for indefinite periods of time. At one time, Hela, goddess of the dead, usurped the rule of Valhalla, despite the fact it was on a different dimensional plane than Hel (see *Hela*). Odin has since reclaimed the land. The ninth of the Nine Worlds is *Muspelheim*, land of the fiery demons. Until his recent disappearance, the primordial demon Surter ruled Muspelheim. Muspelheim is on its own dimensional plane, separate from all the other Nine Worlds. In the Asgardians' account of the origin of their cosmology, Muspelheim, the land of fire, and Nifleheim, the land of ice, were said to predate recorded time, separated from one another by Ginnungagap, the Yawning Void.

Asgard is honeycombed with nexus-portals to the various extradimensional realms of the Nine Worlds, making the worlds (with the exception of Earth) sometimes seem like they are on a contiguous plain. (Indeed, early cartographers of Asgard mapped it this way.) The only permanent portal to Earth, *Bifrost*, the Rainbow Bridge, has recently been shattered, severing Asgard's connection with Earth and making passage between realms difficult. There is a special passageway from Asgard to the extradimensional realm of Olympus, home of the Greek gods (see *Olympus*). Since Olympus is not a part of the Asgardian cosmology, this nexus-portal is believed to be an artificial rather than natural phenomenon. Another unique feature of Asgard is the Cave of Time, an apparently natural phenomenon through which passage to other time eras is possible.

It is probable that somewhere in Asgard's outlying Sea of Space there are floating nexus-portals to Earth's space. Beings of the Earthly dimension have in certain instances been able to travel from Earthly to Asgardian space. There may indeed be an edge to Asgard's Sea of Space, perhaps at the perimeter of the "Dome of the Sky" extending from the outer edge of ringed Jotunheim. At the edge of the Sea there would exist "dimensional borderlands" which serve as transitional areas between discrete dimensions.

Asgard and its sister realms are populated by six distinct humanoid races, described under *Asgardians*. Besides these, there are several singular creatures who exist upon various of the Nine Worlds. The first is the Midgard Serpent Jormungand, an immense snake-like dragon whose body encircles the inner edge of the mountains of Jotunheim closest to Midgard. The Midgard Serpent lies at the very edge of the dimensional boundary between Jotunheim and Midgard, and prevents passage between dimensions. The second is the winged dragon Nidhogg, who lives in Niffleheim and gnaws at one of the roots of Yggdrasil. The third is the giant wolf-god Fenris, who is responsible for the war-god Tyr's loss of a hand. Fenris is imprisoned in the distant land of Varinheim. The fourth creature is the primordial ice giant Ymir (see *Ymir*).

First appearance: JOURNEY INTO MYSTERY #85.

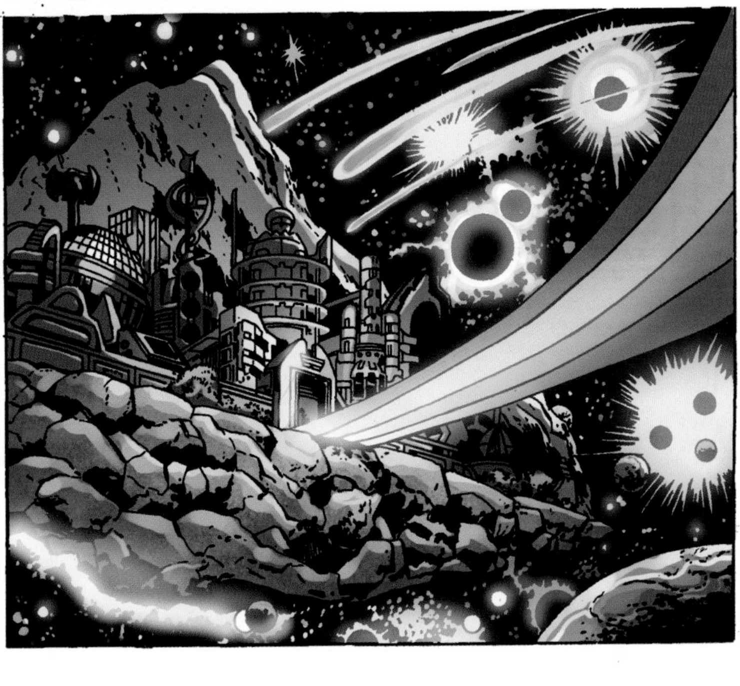

THOR'S HAMMER

Thor wields the enchanted hammer named Mjolnir, one of the most formidable weapons known to man or god. Forged out of the mystical metal uru, whose chief properties are durability and ability to maintain enchantment, the hammer is 2 feet long and its handle is wrapped in leather which terminates in a thong. Besides being a nearly indestructible throwing weapon, the hammer has been given six enchantments by Odin to augment its physical qualities.

The *first* enchantment is that no living being can lift the hammer from the ground unless he or she is worthy. Provisions to that enchantment require that there can be but one worthy wielder of the hammer at a given time, and the current wielder must be bested in fair combat by a worthy contestant in order for that contestant to win it. The *second* enchantment causes the hammer to return to the exact spot from which it is thrown after striking its target. The *third* enchantment enables its wielder to summon the elements of storm (wind, rain, thunder, and lightning) by stamping its handle once on the ground. The *fourth* enchantment enables the hammer to open interdimensional portals, allowing its wielder to travel to other dimensions, such as from Earth to Asgard. (It is not known how Thor determines which dimension he wishes to travel to.) The *fifth* enchantment, given the hammer by Odin in recent times, enables Thor to transform into the guise of a mortal, physician Donald Blake, by stamping the hammer's head to the ground twice. A provision of this enchantment requires that the hammer can not be out of Thor's hand for more than one minute without his spontaneous reversion to his mortal self. When Thor transforms to Blake, his hammer takes the appearance of a gnarled wooden walking stick. So disguised, the hammer's enchantments limiting those who could lift it are not in effect.

The hammer has had one enchantment that has been rescinded. Formerly the hammer could be swung in such a way as to generate chronal displacement inertia enabling its wielder to travel through time. This property, discrete from the hammer's dimension-spanning ability, was recently taken away by Immortus (see *Immortus*), whose mastery over time exceeds that of the gods themselves.

By throwing the hammer and grasping its leather thong, Thor can magically propel himself through the air in the semblance of flight. Just as the hammer can magically change its course in order to return to his hand when he threw it, so can it be influenced by its wielder to change its course while it was in his grasp. The precise manner in which Thor "steers" his hammer while in flight is not known, nor is the precise speed and distance Thor can attain with a single throw. Thor has been observed to be able to attain escape velocity from Earth's gravity with a single throw and to overtake space vessels.

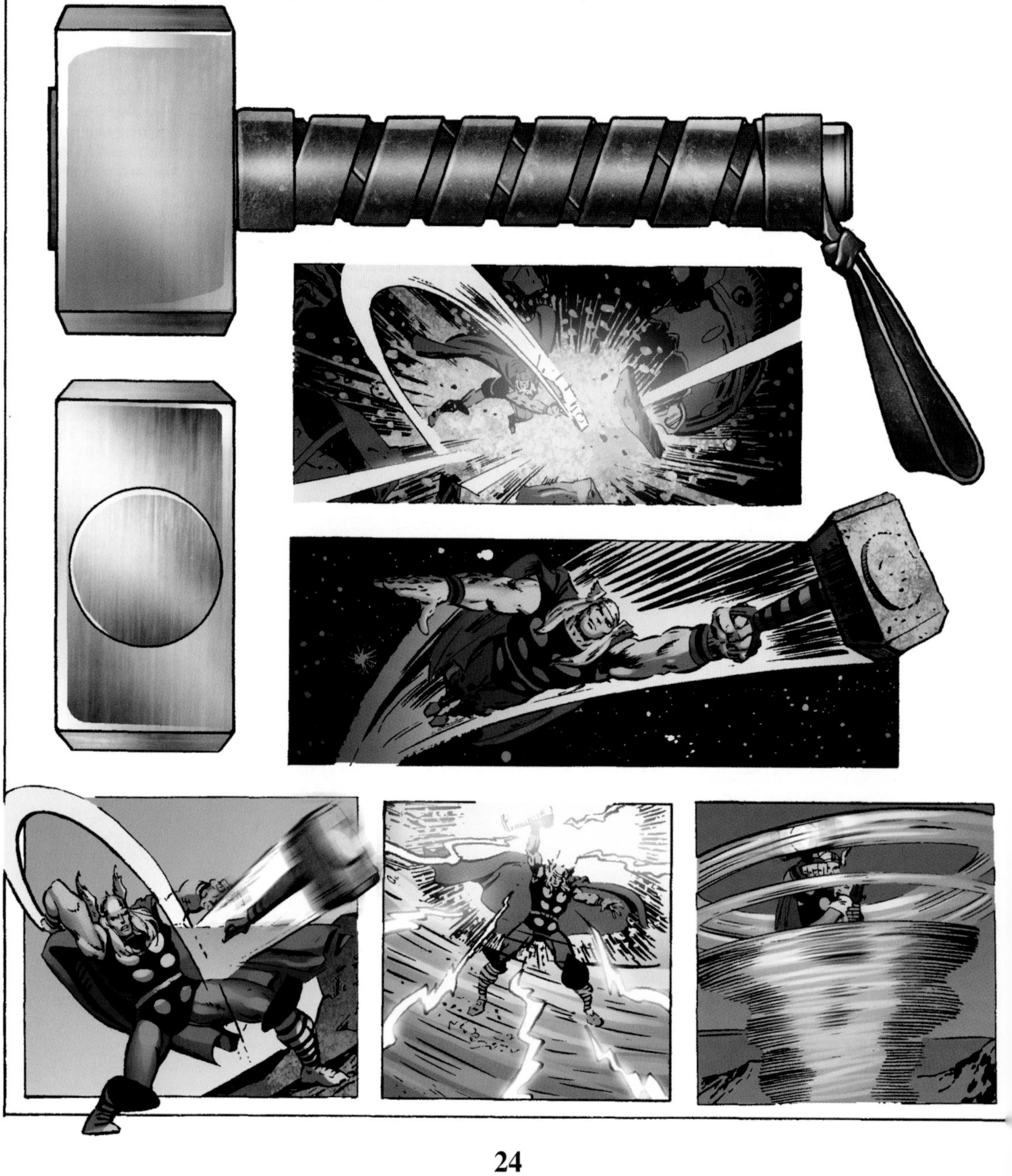